Frankenstein's Paradox

Other works from Casa Forte Press

Mayflower II
Sketches from a Lost Age
by Peter Padfield

Vultures In My Living Room
by Lula Falcão

The Work
by JD Hollingsworth

Frankenstein's PARADOX

or
The Spring Valley Ape

JD Hollingsworth

Copyright © 2014, 2019 by JD Hollingsworth

All rights reserved. No part of this book may be used or reproduced in any manner whatsoever without written permission except in the case of brief quotations embodied in critical articles or reviews.

This book is a work of fiction. Names, characters, businesses, organizations, places, events and incidents either are the product of the author's imagination or are used fictitiously. Any resemblance to actual persons, living or dead, events, or locales is entirely coincidental.

For information contact:

Casa Forte Press
995 Forrest Blvd
Decatur, GA 30030

www.casafortepress.com

Book and cover design by the author

ISBN 978-1-54399-743-9

Printed in the United States of America.

First Edition: November 2019

10 9 8 7 6 5 4 3 2 1

CASA FORTE
PRESS

To

Burt Reynolds

Special acknowledgement to Rand Raynor

*"Dreams are meant to be exactly what they are.
A dream."*

- Nature Boy, Ric Flair

I

JD Hollingsworth

"**B**ogs."
It thought.

"Oxbows."
It thought.

"But... not a decent *natural* lake in Georgia... "

What Am I was too freshly formed to yet have identity, though still so aware as to feel it also unnatural when it opened its eyes, to find it was being kissed, deeply and passionately, by a large, naked, and barrel-chested Man with a vast gray beard whose great bald head was compassed by a spiked and radiant crown of blinding sunlight. The Man rose up on his knees and, nigh weeping with joy, gazed down upon *What Am I* with the adorational beholding of a triumphant artist, then around to the breechclothed and tunicated pantheon in attendance, which raised its hands in ovation and its voice in huzzahs. Like a splendid, perfect and blue-patinated sea-god of some grand and ancient fountain, *What Am I* issued forth a glittering spout from its cobalt lips and the World spun with *What Am I* as its axis. Pajamaed bearers came forth to convey glorious *What Am I* upon a litter to a magnificent awaiting coach, which ferried it afar to a fanfare of trumpets.

What Am I might have thought this an exceedingly strange dream were it entering, not exiting, the darkest slumber. And still, *What Am I* did not even know...

who it was.

"I *am* a... *who*... But..."

"Roosevelt...
"Roosevelt!
"Roosevelt Franklin...
"Roosevelt – Delano – Franklin!!"

Yes.

Frankenstein's Paradox

June 27, 1966

The following Monday afternoon, on page three of the *Atlanta Journal,* there appeared a photograph of a large, gray-bearded man in a White Stag Speedo kneeling over a recumbent teen and surrounded by bathers, captioned,

> Unidentified man administers life-giving mouth-to-mouth resuscitation to R.D. Franklin (16) of Utinahica on the beach at Lake Spivey. Franklin was rendered unconscious while participating with other teens in a contest of "chicken" Saturday afternoon during an outing at the popular Atlanta-area destination. Several days of high temperatures and Sunday's Atlanta 300 at nearby Atlanta Motor Speedway (win to Mario Andretti: See *Sports*) brought record numbers to the lake this past weekend. Franklin was inanimate in the water for an extent of time according to witnesses. The boy sustained additional injuries, including broken ribs, and is recovering at Grady Hospital.
> (*Photo: Alvin Samples Jr.*)

After that Saturday, Roosevelt Delano Franklin was never quite the same. He had always been bright, gifted even, and his mental capacities were undiminished, yet, after being pulled from the mud and the void, he had been reborn with poor impulse control: prone to sudden, over-reactive, fits of dander that, all too often, left him on the side of actions that were not – to be straight up – in his best interest.

***

JD Hollingsworth

October, 1973

No one here called Roosevelt Delano Franklin by his given name anymore. Now, in this place, they called him, "Gator." Perhaps this was due to his most recent arrest: the very one which accounted for his being a guest of the state; the one that had three Ware County deputies pulling him from the Okefenokee over near Waycross – fighting and snapping – after bolting from a logging crew. It was just as likely his reptilian byname emerged from the recent film, *White Lightning*, featuring Burt Reynolds, whom Franklin more than a mite resembled.

Whatever the reason, it was Gator Franklin who stood in the exercise yard of the Georgia State Prison at Reidsville watching a crew of street-clothed men pulling cables and setting up lights, while others – costumed pretenders to his bound fellows – milled freely about, smoking and drinking coffee beyond the fence that caged them.

Coincidentally, one of the men on the other side of the fence *was* Burt Reynolds – location filming at the penitentiary – and Gator stood by the wire, holding the back of his hand to his forehead and squinting in defiance of the glaring sun, hoping to spy his near *doppelgänger* among the film crew. Spotting Eddie Albert loitering near the fence, Gator gripped the chain link, pressed his mustache to the wire and through a rhomboidal void called, "*Ahhh-leee-vahhhhhr!*"

Albert looked his way, gave him a thumbs-up, smiling, then, frowning, turned to move further away.

"*Ha*, that's fuckin' hilarious..." Gator said to no one, then sauntered back to a group of inmates standing around a weight bench.

"... But know what *is* funny?"

"*Huh?*"

"This shit's calmed the place down..."

"...Ya *know* that Ollie dude?"

"No."

***

There were at least three other inmates from Utinahica at Reidsville. There was Jericho Milton, who had fled for his life from there fourteen years before for a crime he did not commit and was, for a time, forced to live a life of larcenies – petty and grand – to survive. He redeemed himself in the church and worked his way up from mowing lawns to owning a successful landscaping company. With his life finally in order, Jericho ended up in Reidsville for being the black man nearest another crime he did not commit. One thing he was sure of, though: he was still far better off than had he stayed in Utinahica that long-ago day. Now he had made of himself a shot caller and the institutional organizer for the Reidsville chapter of the Black Guerilla Family.

And there were the Duquesnes: Rafe Reilman "Rifleman" Duquesne and his twin brother Rail Road, who, despite having the best prison nickname as his actual, true and given birth name, was, for some reason, known only as "Pie." The person who did know why was Tyrell Dante "Backhoe" Buchanan who, while shuffling and jangling along to isolation in his four-piece suit, passed Rail Road and cried, "HA! You pie! Pie are square! No! *Cornbread* are square, pie are *round!* HA HAhahahahaha!!!"

Backhoe was shanked the day he returned to the general population and the mystery, it seemed, died with him but the name stuck like *meringue*.

"Ya know, Pie..." Gator mused to the rooster-cut brother, "next ta bein' a engineer... think I'd like ta be a... a *movie* star..."

"Shit, dumbass, who wudn't," Pie sagely observed.

"No, asshole, I mean it... *I* could be a actor."

"Well, go o'er yonder an' act..."

"Tried ta be a extra..."

"Extry whut?"

"*A extra...* in the movie... Said they wouldn't be allowin' any 'vi-o-lent *o*-ffenders.'"

"Shiiiiit. Sorry, buddy peg. Well, ya kin still drive trains when ya git out."

"Fuck, Pie... *Engineer*." Gator shook his head in exasperation. "Again... *Jesus*...Buildin' highways an' bridges, stadiums... Hell, jus' do... somethin' what matters. Permanent. A trans-oceanic tunnel... be part of a big dam... ya know, part a somethin' what'll be there... forever."

"Gotta go ta schoolin' fer tha' shit..."

"... Went ta Tech... two quarters."

"*No* shit? Wuh' happ'n'd?"

"Knocked out a professor..."

"*HA-Haa!*" Pie honked like a foghorn, "You *always* aggervated dog... Always wi'tha drama. What *you* needs ta git's a atta-*toood* adjus'ment!"

"Got adjusted. That's the problem..."

"You say so..." Pie sighed with resignation and stepped on an ant.

"For a while there... was thinkin' a bein' a doctor, did some pre-med... but..." Gator trailed off.

"Smarts run'n th'fambly?"

"Ha. Yeah, right. Well, ol' man had a P-H-D."

"No shit?"

"Yeah... *post hole digger*... Poor bastard spent thirty years diggin' his own grave with it."

Pie scowled, nodded pensively and gravely observed, "Yeah...reckon that'd take a looong time a-usin' one a them... But you'd a-gotta shave though."

"*What?*"

"Be a movie star. You'd a-gotta shave off that big-ass pussy duster offa yer face, buddy peg..." Pie said, slowly dragging his tattooed knuckle across his own mustache as if savoring some long-lingered aroma. "Ain't none a 'em got no mustaches no more... Ya know? I mean," and he pointed through the fence, "lookit Burt Reynolds..."

***

Just beyond the guard gate, on the lintel above the entry to the institution, and where its single, fleeting observation could have the least inspirational impact on the fresh fish riding chain into the penitentiary – with only the rape they were incessantly reminded of on their minds – is displayed Julian Hoke Harris' Deco/Egyptian low-relief frieze, "Rehabilitation." Upon its carved stone, flanking the seated embodiment of scale-wielding Justice (who here, in this most – demographically speaking – homo-sexual of places, is male) are figures representing the trades, crafts, agriculture, and sports.

Following up on the artwork's promise, the Georgia Department of Offender Rehabilitation provided training in a variety of careers and skills. Seeing himself as a modernized Paul Muni engineer/convict in *I Am a Fugitive from a Chain Gang,* Gator Franklin became a "programmer," faithfully participating in general clerk and building maintenance classes he hoped could be a foot on the path to carry him back to Georgia Tech, and he did his best to become a model inmate: "No smoke."

Aside from what everyone assumed, though, the "brake fluid," as they called it, (the medications – the indiscriminate cocktail of anti-epileptics and downers pushed in the pill line: the secobarbital, phenytoin, oxcarbazepine, the methaqualone and diazepam) was having no effect. No effect because they were puked up or thrown away when possible for making him lazy and insane. He *had*, though, found some success in suppressing his prehistoric hindbrain through artistic endeavors – constructing collages and such – and in meditation. And the pill pushers – attributing his new self-control to their "fluid," and mostly indifferent, anyway – didn't check his mouth too carefully.

So, he was on his best behavior shooting for parole, and it truly was *his* behavior: controlled and un-pharmacologically altered.

His anoxic brain injury, though, especially in this place, had led to incidents he knew could be a struggle to overcome for the review board if he wanted an early release.

As Rifleman explains,

"Mane, time he a-flat-weeded that fuh-ckin' lop a-doin' Scribble... that shit were *fuuuuucked* up, mane. Reckon th' brake fluid they a-gots'im on done knocked tha' shit out, mane, bu' shit bro, he'da kep' tha' shit up he'd a-been a-lookin' at fuckin' *Buck* Rogers time!"

Or, more clearly: Six months after his arrival at Reidsville – when he was still "Franky" or "Book," and in far less control of his reactions – Gator had engaged some "knucklehead" Forrest Knight in a game of Scrabble. Gator had let pass such egregious affronts as the knucklehead's use of the word "kiln," which, in spite of the following exchange –

"So... ya actually know what a *'kiln'* is?"

"Fuck yeah, motherfucker! I knows all 'bout *a-kiln!*"

"Kiln," as in "murdering" – Gator had allowed this unchallenged, as it *was* still a word. And he held his breath and counted to ten when the Knight questioned Gator's use of the word "lava" since it was a kind of soap – a proper name: "Like ya cain't say, "Pal-*fuckin'*-molive!"

Gator calmly pointed out that the soap was called that because of pumice and the Knight relented since he, for reasons known only to him, thought pumice to be some sex or genitalia disease-related word and it made him giggle.

Yet, after Gator cleared his own rack of S,S,D,E,L,U, and P playing across the bottom row to expand the word "PO" to the left with an S, U, and P, and continuing rightward adding an S, followed by the existing terminal E in a vertical "FAILURE," then his remaining D, L and Y of his rack to spell "SUPPOSEDLY" (with a triple word bonus, including double letter bonuses for the U and Y in that word, *and* in the additionally formed "QUIPU" – from a vertical "QUIP" (with a blank tile as its P) – and "ALLY" – from a vertical "ALL" – along with *their* additional word values, a triple word bonus for the word "AS" formed from the middle S on the triple word block and an existing A above it, *and* a fifty point bonus for clearing his rack) the knucklehead Knight challenged Gator, condescendingly, that the word was not "supposedly" but "suppose-*ably*," only to find himself on the floor with a broken jaw.

And, of course, such continued behavior would, as Rifleman's euphemism implied, lead to Gator's imprisonment into the 25th century.

Still, recalling this, even years later – as he was at this moment – would enrage Gator's amygdala forcing a great struggle to maintain. He hoped to discover some coping mechanism like the shrink in the "ding wing" had suggested: some deep mental exercise to arrest the flash impulses of his reptile brain to strike; to allow the neurotransmitters to equilibrate their release and reuptake – or, as Gator liked to say, "for my 'brain squeezin's' ta get their shit together."

Meanwhile, he still felt not just angry, but justified, regarding the incident. "One-*HUN*-dred-*FIFTY* fuckin' points! Illiterate fuckin' peckerwood..." he would occasionally grumble aloud. It wasn't the points really, though, or even the challenge, it was just that the knucklehead just didn't know the word.

And he felt remorse.

"Awrite, buddy peg, jes' got two caps fer four books," Pie re-entered Gator's brain to announce. "Wanna hit?"

"Whu..." Gator blurted returning to the moment. "Oh... No can do, *hombre*... Anyways, I need ta talk ta somebody."

"Sheeeeeiiiiit, *dog*..."

Gator walked across the yard to where Jericho Milton was addressing the Family with a group of prospective recruits. Gator stood at a distance, but near the edge of the audience, waiting.

Listening.

"...if you talk the talk but only walk so lightly as ta fall behind, ta sink an' wallow in a mire of pleasure, an' not ta march for th'advancement a the revolution, then you are on a *per*-sonal *trip*, brother, an' there is *no truth* in your struggle. Brother, you can *not* be a part of society an' aim ta destroy it. You can *not* be a part a *this* thing an' desire the poison fruits a the tree a this *so*-ciety... The socially conditioned cannot advance the destruction a society's status quo – the *ways a the people* bein' society's ways... Brother, we do *not* seek ta *change* society, ta *improve* society... ta advance *so-ciety* in any way, but ta advance the re-vo-lution. An' *only* the revolution.

"Society must be wiped clean away. Brother, misguided compassion for what *is,* merely preserves what is *ripe – for – destruction.* Before the new can live, the old must die, brother, an' it is our single-minded... altruistic... self-*sacrificing* objective ta break *down* this paradigm, ta shatter... ta *lynch* it, burn an' bury it so a new one may take *root.*

"We don't look ta change, brother... not ta change, but *uncompromisin' destruction!"*

"Yes!" "You know it!" "Truth, man! Truth!" the congregation cheered in accordance.

"Uncompromisin' destruction!"

"Right on!" "Tell it the way it is Jer'cho!"

"*Un-com-pro-misin' – De-struction!"*

"Tha's right, brother, tha's right!" "Uh huh!"

Gator started to clap, thought better of it, then put his hands back down as Jericho continued.

"In this lawless place a lawless men we know a *one* law, the *only law,* the Law a Nature, brother, the privilege a the stronger... That *the – weak – are – devoured – by – the – strong...* In the ladder a order an' rank, the bourgeoisie are weak grafters, living off the labor a the strong, broad masses... "

Milton spied Gator leaning against the wall nearby and without removing his gaze continued, irritated, "The aggressive man, bein' the stronger, the bolder... the nobler, has *at all times* the better view, the clearer conscience on his side, an' in the END, what will *pre*-vail?"

Milton returned his attention to the gathered recruits, "The strength! The boldness! The nobility a the righteous!

"When such time comes – an' it will – the *will ta power!* the will ta *life!...* when such time comes – an' it will – the *will ta power!* the instict ta *freedom!...* when such time comes – an' it will – *the will ta power!* the wrath a the *be-liever!...* will be *dead*-lier than the *might* a the o-ppressor!"

The crowd nodded to one another and rumbled, menacingly.

"But for *now...* we cannot take the fight ta where it needs ta go, my brothers. In here all we can do is talk... an' plan... an' wait. But, so we can be ready *when* that day comes, we have one mission: *ta* SURVIVE!"

"You know it!" "Sur-vive!" the crowd replied and cheered.

"Survival, pendin' revolution, my brothers. Survival, pendin' revolution."

"*Yes, motherfucker!*" "*GODdamn truth!*" "*Right fuckin' on, brother!*"

Jericho Milton stepped out to wander among his people. He roamed his crew, shaking hands, hugging and now and then throwing a less than pleased glance at Gator, who still leaned against the wall, smiling.

After a few more minutes Milton said, "'Scuse me, my brothers..." and broke away to where Gator waited.

"Heavy shit man..." Gator drolly, yet sincerely complimented. "Burn the place down for a greater good. Strength through self-overcomin' an' sublimation... Like... Nietzsche... with soul. But, yeah, I'm down with it..."

"Whatcha want 'wood?" Milton snapped sharply.

"Maannn... I ain't no peckerwood. You *know* me..."

"All peckerwoods... 'Least y'ain't no Knight... an'... *again*, what-is-it-that-you-want?"

"Okay... So, you're the best jailhouse lawyer in this place an' I was wonderin' you could... help me with my parole hearin', get ready, when I get one."

"Can't do it." Jericho flatly dismissed.

"Really... that the way it is?"

"The way it is 'cause you probably never gonna get no hearin'."

"Why the hell would *I* not get a hearin'? An' how would you *know* that?"

"Because you're ign'rant."

"*What?*"

"Nobody *owed* no hearin' in Georgia." Jericho lectured him on the way it was. "*No* prisoner owed no hearin'. Ain't how it's done in the *Pee*-nut state. S'all behind closed doors. You don't even know you *gettin'* reviewed. All happen without y'involvement. So, couldn't help ya... even'f'I wanted ta... an' anyways, on that note, I no longer assist Mr. Charlie with his baggage."

"Goddamn, that ain't right... 'bout the hearin', I mean..."

"Revolution... 'wood."

"Shit... alright...damn..." Gator held out his fist.

"Can't dap..." Jericho Milton walked away.

Gator stood with his fist out, like a man whose ice cream had dropped from his cone.

***

Frankenstein's Paradox

October, 1974

  Gator sat in the chow hall, paying no attention to his meal or the cacophony around him, staring at the clock, seeing who would blink first.
  He stared until all around it had dissolved into a pale nothingness that hummed with a low white noise and now the clock itself was sinking below the fog's surface.
  He stared until the hands that marked the hours and the minutes and the seconds were things of the past.
  He wished that he could stare time itself into nothingness but knew that time would not cease to exist simply because the mechanism that recorded its passing had been gazed away. Still, he stared and he wondered what time it would be when he would leave all this behind: when he would be free; when he could go on to make something of himself; when...
  "Long time, brother..."
  Gator blinked and the clock bobbed back to the surface.
  "Still here, huh?" the voice asked.
  Gator looked up, then up some more and agreed, "Few more years yet, bu*t you're* late."
  "*Five minutes!*" the guard called.
  "Nuh-uh, Book, right on time. Always, heheheh" the big inmate laughed as he sat down to the long table.
  "Damn. You been out a while this time... an' it's *'Gator'* now... ain't 'Book,'"
  "Huh?"
  "Name..."
  "*Gator?*"

"Yeah, I dunno... somethin' ta do with... Burt Reynolds," Gator sighed.

"Oh... Yeah, man...Sure. Yeah. Reckon I sees that... Ya didn't have no 'stache..."

"So...you're back... " Gator said, stating the obvious. "I mean... obviously... Why?"

"I gots pimpulses."

"Sounds 'bout right."

"Yeah, this my secon' home."

"How's the first? Atlanta?"

"'S'all good, man. All good."

"Happened t'your hand?" Gator nodded towards the new inmate's beefy paw and poked at his chicken cutlet.

"Huh?" The big man looked at the gauze that wrapped his hand. "Oh. Shot..."

"Shot? *Who?*"

The big inmate stared at Gator with a look of utter confoundment, then bellowed, "*Ol' lady*! Man, what, you *serious?*" scowling and shaking his head.

"Right... Of course..."

"Course *she* ain't in no lockup..."

"Mmm nnnnn," Gator grunted in apparent but half-hearted agreement while trying to force a few bites down before the trays got dumped.

"Yeah, you seen her... Time what she come fer th' con'j'gul," the big man said staring off to some point beyond the ceiling where he could see her. "Yes, suh. Sumpin' else..."

"Yeah... she's... alright."

"*Awright?* Man, she-is-*fine!* You seen. Got that wiggle... from workin' down th' car wash."

"Yeah...That one... jus' never gets old..." Gator mumbled brusquely and pushed his tray away.

"Say," the old lifer next to Gator leaned in to interrupt, "Ya gonna finish that there portion?" and bobbed his head at Gator's tray.

Gator looked down at the gray-yellow slab and laughed, "Nah, man. Go for it... S*'alllll* you Cap'n!"

"Y'ole lady ain't never shot you?" the big man went back into it.

"Uhhhhh. No."

"No foolin'?"

"Nah, but, really, I try ta... avoid gettin'... attached. Kinda better for everybody..."

"*Hmmmm*...Don't say..." the inmate pondered then

proclaimed, "*Good Book* say, 'An' th'lord God sezeth, ain't good what a man should oughta be alone; I will make him an help meet fuh him.'"

"Right."

"Fuh this th'will a God, even what ya be sanctified, that y'all *abstain* from *FOR*-ni-cation."

"Well, least I'm doin' *that* part right."

"An' whoso findeth a wife findeth a good thang, an' obtaineth favour a th'lord!"

"Yeah... I don't know 'bout that hap'nin'..."

"Lid fuh ev'ry pot, bro'..."

"*Three minutes!*" the guard called.

"Think I need a different kinda... help..." Gator turned his head to look around the room and at the guards, "an' I don't think it's th' lord's what's watchin' anyways."

"Always lookin' out, maybe you don't see – like th' man what got no boat."

"This one a your... parables?"

"Jus' a story, bro. Man stuck in a flood sittin' on 'is porch... canoe come by, say, 'hop on in, getcha back to dry land,' an' he say, 'No, I'm-a prayin' fuh th' lord ta save me' an'..."

"Yeah," Gator interrupted the parable to synopsize, "flood gets worse, an' a boat an' a helicopter... Guy drowns asks... Jesus or whatever, why you didn't save my ass an' Jesus says 'I sent ya two boats and a helicopter...' Yeah, Arlene used ta tell that story... thought it would inspire me."

"Jus' a-sayin' what th'lord don't show 'is hand. Maybe. Jus' a-sayin' what th'lord stepping in an' ya ain't know it. Or maybe it ain't time... yet. He step in when the time... right. Fuh real, like."

"I was jus' won'drin' when that would be. What time."

"No, motherfucker... it ain't time..."

"*One minute!*" the guard called.

"Now ain't th' time," the big inmate sermonized on. "Hence th' fall *no* man know th' time. Not 'til the day a th' Beast. Don't know when *IS*... ain't no gamblin' man, but this... this not yet th' time. You know when th' time come. 'Day a th' Lord so cometh as a *thief* in th' night. Fuh when they says, 'peace an' safety...' *THEN* sudden destruction *cometh* upon 'em...' day ya comes ta knowledge... day what thou eatest thereof, thou shalt surely die."

"Oh–Kay..."

"Meantime, *you* always lands on ya feet."

"*Me?*..." Gator burst in astonishment. "Ha... Okay... Yeah, well, I *land*... *MEAN*time... tired a always spinnin' in the air. Tired a gettin' nowhere... a bein'... nothin'."

"Nothin'? Right time a day, any man cast a *loooong* shadow."

"Yeah, right before it gets dark."

"He done 'pointed th' moon fuh th' seasons an' lucky ol' sun knoweth his *goin' down*. He maketh darkness, an' it is night: wherein all th' beasts a th' forest do *creep* forth."

"I got *no* idea what you're tryin' to say, Preacher..." Gator laughed.

The big inmate appeared lost in thought, then blinked, shook his head and said, "Anyways, 12:01 only time what matter... Still playin' Scrapple?"

"Dump your trays!"

***

Frankenstein's Paradox

<u>*May, 1975*</u>

> *...I understand that, as part of my supervision, my parole officer or any other parole officer may, at any time, conduct a warrantless search of my person, papers, place of residence, automobile or any other property under my control. I will maintain gainful employment or, upon the directive of my Parole Officer, pursue a general education diploma (GED high school diploma), or vocational/technical school trade...*

Roosevelt Delano Franklin read through the document that would, any time now, make him a free man. All of his concern about parole reviews and the Scrabble incident were moot because, in order to make room for more marijuana smokers in the prison system, inmates of all stripes were being paroled willy-nilly. After he was out, all Gator had to do was walk down paper for the remainder of his sentence. Until that time he would have to keep it together, keep his nose clean, follow the rules for his PO.

After that he would then, and for all time, be a free man.

***

Gator turned down the hall outside the john, that spot where no one could get a good look at what was happening: at least not the guards. He stopped to light a cigarette and at first heard, then saw the commotion. A couple of Knights had a new inmate against the dark corner and were taking turns. The new man's muffled cries were pathetic: the shock of the new. Soon enough they would change. As the weeks, the months, the years wore on, they would become stronger, angrier, but still muffled and still have no effect.

Gator stood watching and the Knight who was having his way at that moment turned to see him. The Knight put two fingers to his eyes then pointed them at Gator. The rapist was telling Gator that *he* was the one being seen, being busted, not the Knight nor his actions.

Gator hated to see the weak get picked on, hated to see things cry, but told himself it was not his business who was "ballin' the fish." He was not going to intervene. That was a fool's errand. There was no point in getting himself in this: it would only make it bad for the both of them.

Not now, for sure. It was too close, and, anyway, everybody got it eventually.

And Gator told himself what everybody knew: no one knew what happens back there.

***

Frankenstein's Paradox

<u>*June, 1975*</u>

The guard's and Gator's footfalls echoed off the concrete and steel all around as he strolled like a boss down the line of cells beyond his for the last time. An open hand slid through the bars as he passed.
"Time is it, buddy peg?" Rifleman's hand asked.
"Twelve – *O* – one…"
Their palms touched as he passed, fingers sliding across one another's until they drew apart and the distance between them grew as he walked on down the catwalk to freedom.
"Ah *heard* that…
 …Later…

 …Tell Screwy ah said, *'heh-loooww'*…

 …Love ya brotherrrr!"

***

II

JD Hollingsworth

August, 1975

After out-processing, Gator lived the life he was required to arrange before leaving the joint. So, now, at the Wise Acres Mobile Park, he lived in "the trailer of the mother" with the immobile Arlene Franklin and her forever-parked paramour, the wheelchair-bound Tarpley Skeeve, within their singlewide prefab. There, subsisting on welfare, food stamps, Social Security and Skeeve's disability, the elder couple never, except to use the bathroom – and not always then – left the "living room" and the flickering blue light of its television, much less the trailer.

This was all awful, though it did mean Gator had a room of his own, and on the evening of the first day he beheld that in that room there was a light switch. After more than three years of never being allowed the most simple dignity of turning any light on or off, of never having the light divided from the darkness by his own command, three years of powerlessness, now, within this cube *from which* the World could be locked *out* – not him *in* – he ruled over the night and over the day. It was fulfilling, empowering: ennobling. He snapped the grimy, grease smudged and blackened toggle over and over. At times he held the darkness for a while, savoring its cool wisdom and mystery, then, having no more of its impenetrable philosophy, in a flash, sent it scurrying, like the vermin that gathered within it, by the might of plain and simple knowledge. Other times he detained the light with its oh-so-full-of-itself know-it-all-ness and busybody prying, only to chase its peeping with a cold bucket of indignant unknown.

All as he alone saw fit.

Still, in that trailer, in that little room, bound by the four faux-pine plastic wallboards that defined it, with its lauan, hollow core door pulled tight against Skeeve, his mother and television, and though its bolt did hold the awfulness beyond out, as time passed, too many of the desperate, hopeless feelings of those previous years returned there.

So, switch or not, he surrendered his simple control – the rule that he there held supreme – and spent most of his time just not being there, not exacting that rule at all.

From his own agonizing personal history, Gator was acutely aware that alcohol only made his limbic reactions more likely and more terrible. State-imposed interdiction against its use until he ran out his sentence aside, now, outside the safe containment of prison walls, Gator also knew that any altercation before he cleared paper, and probably even after, would return him instantly back to within those walls, and he would have none of that: ethanol would not fuel a trip back there. So, though for now he remained a teetotaler, still, he did spend a great deal of his free time not drinking at the God I'm Gonna Miss Her Bait & Tackle Shop: an actual bait shop, transformed after four o'clock every afternoon, except Sunday, into a honky-tonk roadhouse, with live music from the 441 White Line Fevers three nights a week.

"Miss Her" was the only show in town for socializing, even though, with its bubbling green-water tanks of polliwogs, creek chubs, and leeches, and compost-filled tubs of fat, mucus-buttered nightcrawlers, some might say the place smelled sort of awful. But this was not the case, for humans, though a fussy bunch, will acclimate to anything, then call that funk their own. Or, let us say, embrace the familiar, and to the country and woodland folk of Utinahica, the moist and life-revealing funk of Nature was ever so familiar and an appreciated and soothing balm. So, evening after evening, the lonely, the horny, the angry and the thirsty gathered to court and spark, serenaded by the bait crickets trill, as if on a moonlit picnic, abreast a babbling forest brook redolent of life's bouquet.

The bait and tackle was also sanctuary not only from the sepulchral singlewide of Wise Acres and his own solitary existence, but from Gator's job as well. The only work he could arrange from prison was with the roofing company owned by a friend of Arlene's neighbor in the trailer park, and it was commercial work: so, all flat roofs. Very little work is as disagreeable as mopping molten hot tar on black roofs in the beating sun of the Georgia summertime. This alone was crushing to mind and body, but, adding misfits to misery, those he worked with were, in his opinion, the dumbest crackers he had ever known – and having spent three years in the Georgia state prison system, this was saying something.

So, though not bound by the physical steel, stone and stringently, savagely, enforced submission of prison, where deliverance was found only at the end of a long and slowly passing funereal parade of years, Gator still found that each day held its own despair and misery in fruitless repetition, devoid of joy or comfort and from which escape seemed equally improbable.

How long would it be, if ever, until he could get out, move on, move up?

What could he do, if anything, in the interim to change or mitigate, these irritations, these perpetual routines?

"What botherations," he lamented, and, before returning to the trailer park after work, sat a while at Miss Her, sipping a Shasta cola, listening to the cricket's song, and watching the big jar of pink pickled sausage on the counter. He screwed up his face, nodded, and said, "Well, I know I can figure *this* out," and decided to hang tough for now: to stick with it until the conundrums and necessary actions that lay before him could be correctly analyzed.

Gator peered into the greasy glass jug which, with its embalmed contents, reminded him of some antique and derelict museum specimen or carnival grotesque. He turned up the raspberry soda, belched silently, and mumbled, "Look at'im go!" cheering on the flushed yet tireless frankfurter that had ceaselessly risen and fallen through its murky solution since Gator had first sat down to consume a hot pink jar-mate he requested be retrieved by a pair of unwashed tongs.

"*Olll'* Red," Gator declared, now on a first-name basis with the unnaturally red sausage that sank gently down to join his brothers lying about like sunburned opium smokers on the bottom. Gator absent-mindedly worked his tongue to remove the stubborn remains of the preparation he had recently chewed and pondered ponderous puzzles.

Ol' Red slowly embarked upon his return to the surface, and Gator brooded over the pickle *he* faced. What could compel him to break out of his stagnancy, what forces, what conditions, what powers could be powerful enough to act upon him in way that would allow him to rise above, trapped as he was? Or just force him to action: to get moving. Why were things the way they were?

"E*ndless*..." Gator observed. "Why...? Cycling... Redundancy. Pointless, but... soluble, I think..."

In school and incarceration, Gator had, long ago, learned how the world was all about rules and laws that guided, like an intelligent hand – or fist – and knew his situation, his *place*, was clear but rigid: non-deformable. And, anyway, this was not manipulation by gamesman spirits: This was... science.

"No. No devil here," Gator thought, as he followed the hot link back to the bottom. Recalling the acuity of a once promising past, Gator reviewed the ambient influences; the empirically knowable agents that not only contained him but could also contribute to his breakout from stasis.

"Well, the damn temper'ture for one. *No, man...* that shit... ain't right," Gator lamented. "It's been the same, like, every fuckin' second. So, that shit ain't changin'. Not quick. So... yeah, fuck that," and reckoned, "Man, *that* shit otta make *ev-er-y* one, move..."

"An' *con*-stant pressure..." Gator said aloud, rubbing his brow. "Always. So, also not good... Not fuckin' changin'. Can't... way things are."

Could unchangeable things be considered, Gator wondered and also surmised that any force that could apply to all, would not work for *him*. Gator knew he was somehow unique. "This guy's diff'rent..." he proudly granted, pointing with his thumb.

The red-hot lifted off and ascended with the gentle grace of an airship and Gator languidly muttered, "*Montgolfier*," in his snootiest French accent.

Down the counter, Randall, the bartender, looked up from his *Guns and Ammo* magazine to ask, "Eh? What? Well, you'll be a...? A *what*? Monkey's uncle*? heheheh*"

Lost in his own analyses, Gator said, "*Gas!* Gas is a thing too... Really, yeah... Keeps goin' up... But can't change that eith-... Or...?"

Still believing he was involved in a conversation, Randall said, "Yeah... *wayy*y up. Way more'n what it were las' year! Twicet's much! Fuck OPEC! AY-rabs!"

Though deaf to the world, Gator still knew it was indeed more than it was before. Right here, right now. "Increases... Goes up, but... all this travelin' around, it sure don't last... Fill up... up... But then it's... gone... Where does it *go?*"

With that in mind, Gator wondered – regardless of how *he* got there – why the rules, the laws, didn't allow him to *just* move *up*. Positivity and consistency should allow for that. "Seems like that's how it *ought* to be."

Then, "But... a-course!" he blurted in revelation. Every time he worked his way up – where tension would be broken, pressure relieved – the rules, the laws, the never-changing way things work, the regulation Gator only now began to understand, made it so he could never *stay* on top. Relief was brief, he would be brought down again. And now he knew why.

Ol' Red descended like a fuchsia bathyscaphe back to the bottom.

"This is... *corruption...*" Gator blurted, popping his fist on the bar. "Soured *eb-u-llition*."

Gator tapped his watch, marking the time that passed, and began to hatch it off on the walls of his mind as he had hatched off the days on those of his cell until, inspired once more, Ol' Red ascended through the brine, bobbing...

Gator tapped his watch again. "Regular... Predictable..." Gator elated. "O-*kay*. Works for me! Gotta go."

Gator moved up out of his seat to head for the door: a slight spring enhanced his step.

"Yeah..." he said poking his finger at Randall as he passed. "So, it's just *that one* fuckin' wiener, one dog what's movin'..." then stopped in his tracks. "Rest a those fuckers just sit there... but *him*, that guy...Up an' down, up an' down... An' it ain't temperature *or* pressure makin' that happen... none a that's changin' in that fuckin' *jar*..."

Randall stood with his mouth catching flies.

"'sides, they'd *allll* be movin' all fuckin' over the place, not jus' him.... Ya know? No fuckin' Car-*teeee*-sian devil, man," Gator declared mockingly. "Nooo. Fermentation! Microbial-Metabolic-Gas-Pro-*duc*tion," he emphasized, syllable-by-syllable, with as many finger jabs. "Bacteria farts, he rises... gas escapes when the surface tension breaks, Ol' Red sinks... Them's the sausage laws!"

"-kay," Randall muttered.

"Repeat... *ad infinitum*..." Gator said dropping a quarter for the soda on the counter and continued on to the door where he stopped again to turn around and say, earnestly, as if correcting him, "Shit ain't *sto*chastic, Randall."

"Nu-uh..." Randall concurred. "Shit ain't."

Gator gave a quick nod and disappeared out to the late afternoon sun that burst in with a blinding flash as the door flew open.

"So, that's all cool," Gator thought, opening the car door. "But, *damn*, yeah... one a these days... I gotta spend some time thinkin' 'bout my *own* shit."

He climbed inside, turned the key, lit a cigarette and stared through the windshield.

"Gotta shake these blues," he thought, suddenly deflated, as he lifted his foot from the brake. "This existential nausea... This... Brownian motion sickness."

He aimed the faded amber Capri towards the Park.

"Now..." he said, blowing a cloud of smoke out the window, "THAT shit's stochastic."

***

Frankenstein's Paradox

Early May, 1976

It had been a year of mopping tar. Gator not only hated the job but was also spending nearly as much as he was bringing home buying new pants and boots to replace the tar-encrusted garb he liked to say made him look like some ice-age sloth pulled from the pits of Rancho La Brea. Not that that oft-repeated line fell upon a single comprehending ear, and this, almost as much as the beating sun and the steaming tar kettle was wearing him down. Still, during lunchtime of the day his parole ended, what was to finally be the last day Gator would *have* to mop tar, he considered remaining at the job until he secured new employment.

But Dwayne Sparks rambled on, "...so we kill tha bong an' then well *she* says 'mah girlfrien's a-comin' over an' she's a-gonna eat my pussy so you needs ta *leave'* an' I says 'kin I watch' an' she says '*NO!* you-*got*-ta-*GO*' an' I says 'well *hell bitch* I slop tar all fu-'"

"Yeah, I'm outta here."

"...Whut?"

"Gone. *Via con Dios, muchacho...* "

"Hell, you cain't jus' leave..."

"Ohhhhhhh, but I can."

Gator gripped the outside of the ladder with his feet, said, "Watch me," and rode it down to the ground like a fireman's pole. He threw his boots in the yard, jumped in the Capri, and drove off in a cloud of blue smoke.

Walking downtown on Railroad Avenue later that day, he saw a pink construction paper sign on a storefront window that read,

HELP! Wanted
General & Maintenance
Possible Advancement
Inquire Within

There was an exasperated, plewding, Magic Marker stick figure drawn next to "HELP!" and the placard's free space was festooned with flowers and smiley faces and peace signs.

Gator looked above him at the façade and saw, "*The Health Hole, Natural Foods, Remedies and Books.*"

"...Health Hole?"

He went inside. It was air-conditioned. The linoleum floor felt good on his stocking feet. He looked around and a sweet-faced hippie girl standing at the register in some kind of pajama get-up asked if she could help him.

"Yeah, the job there?" he asked, pointing his thumb to the door behind him." That still available?"

"Oh-My-God," she said. "I *just* put that on the door! Like, *right now!*"

"Hey...'groovy,' I *just* left my job! Like, *right now!*"

"Oh-My-God, No... Way! That is so... SO amazing," she said with deep, deep sincerity, her hand pressed to her breast.

He, at first, felt as if he should be mocking her, but her genuine amazement and enthusiasm were so refreshing – so *positive* – that he could not help but respond in, un-ironic, kind.

"It really... REALLY is."

"We *really* need a dude – *or* a *chick* – who can take care of things, because Todd..." she held her hand up to the side of her mouth as if letting him in on a secret to whisper, "can *not*," and made a goofy sidelong glance to no one.

"That the owner?"

"Yeah... Mr. Poshlost. *OH!* I should tell him... *Todd! Tooodd!*"

"What!?" came from the back with petulant irritation.

"You are NOT going to *believe* this, but a dude *just* walked in the door 'bout the job. Just walked in..." she looked at Gator with an amazed scowl, "Like, *right now!*"

A dumpy, potato-like man, probably in his thirties with an unkempt but balding mop of Avery Schreiber hair and the weary and rumpled demeanor of a much older a man, came from the back room.

Todd Poshlost, a mediocre Atlanta attorney, had come to Byron for the Atlanta International Pop Festival specifically for Jimi Hendrix – who performed the Star Spangled Banner... on July 4th... *with fireworks*, and all of the alkaloid-derivative-altered in attendance still had minds blown to that day. Todd Poshlost ate Quaaludes and slept through it all in his Fiat. But when he awoke, rubbed his eyes, vomited, and looked around, he had the kind of mind-expanding vision that Quaaludes would reveal and foresaw that south central Georgia would become the Southern equivalent of upstate New York – a pastoral haven for a new generation of artists and musicians and Bohemian poets.

Hearing of Utinahica from a local girl and recognizing its similarity to "Utopia" to be no mere coincidence, he set upon an arduous vanguard journey there, where he then stopped and pointed, Brigham Young-like – and with the same confidence the latter-day Moses must have had when looking down upon the stinking brine pit in the Utah desert – to proclaim, "This is the antipodal post-Woodstock Saugerties." He planted his standard in the cotton-degraded soil of the town of seven hundred and thirty four, and hung up his shingle to handle trailer park restraining orders and canine paternity cases long enough to fund the Health Hole: knowing that the hippies and artists, still yet to arrive but on their way, would need their granolas and tinctures, their sprouts and shark cartilage, Whole Earth Catalogs and Ram Dass books.

"So, yeah, so, you wish to migrate into the program here?" Poshlost droned.

"... You mean... the *maintenance* job?"

"Sure, sure... you might say that," Poshlost sniffed dismissively, then droned on again, "I like to think that we here each wear many hats." He continued with his eyes closed as if reading cue cards off the back of his eyelids, "As we grow, as *we* expand, I want to grok that *you* can expand your involvement at a very high level, not just in the management and overseeing of the facilities complex – HVAC, MEP, refrigeration, various regulatory compliance issues, fire codes, what have you – but to become involved, in a strategically implemented, way, in overseeing, taking ownership of, any programs involving deliverables... I mean, I don't know how granular you'd like your involvement to be but, say... say we move forward with our renovation and expansion plans... We have some really groovy, groovy things about to go down... say, when we begin the big re-envisioning, could you, say, manage a major construction process, one that might involve building up, maximizing our real estate holdings to highest and best use and utilizing our air space to facilitate greater flexibility in our outreach..."

Gator thought, "I know I've been locked away, but... has language changed *this much*?"

"... could you own that through to completion?" the wellness mogul enquired. "And in the expansion of our inventory, and product development... Walk me through this... Walk me through how you would manage our fungibles..."

"Fungibles?" Gator petitioned, "Is that some... health food snack made a mushrooms?"

Poshlost sighed, "*Seriously...* "

"Man... *Sir*... " Gator got serious, "there's a sign on the door 'bout needin' a guy. Right now this is... jus' *this place*, right?" Gator said, gesturing around the space. "I mean this buildin'?"

"I suppose *you* might see it that way... "

"An' it's only one room, mostly... an' the whole buildin's one story..."

"For now..."

"All I can say is..." Gator sighed, felt his mouth going dry, then continued, "I can handle whatever ya got goin' on, brother. I have specific trainin' in buildin' maintenance... general office work, an' studied engineerin' at Tech so..."

"Oh, far out. You're one of the first arrivals. Well, when can you get started?"

"Now."

"Tomorrow. And really, just so you know, I can do every job here... better than anybody. I just can't actually *do* it all. It's not possible for one human. But, like, right now, I have to get back to hanging these shelves, so..." Poshlost impatiently sighed, motioning to a pile of shelf standards and brackets in the back office.

Gator heard the cashier talking to customers in the store, "Oh my God, y'all... these are the *BEST* figs I have ever eaten in my *entire* life!" then he advised, "Think you need to use anchors in that wall, man. Sheetrock..."

"*I think* I know what I'm doing, *thank* you..." Poshlost grunted in barely concealed umbrage. "But... tomorrow, bright and early... at eleven."

Gator nodded, pointing with both hands at Poshlost, and withdrew from the room. As he made his way to the front he looked back over his shoulder to the office several times as if to convince himself what he had experienced was actual, then stopped at the register.

"So... that guy for real?" he asked.

"Oh, yeah, man! *Too real*. Hahaha. If ya know what I mean..." she leaned in, "an' I *think*-ya-*do*. Haha."

"Okay... Well, I start tomorrow, so... I'll see ya in the mornin'."

"Ahhhhh!" she squealed. "That is so far OUT! Yay!"

"Yeah."

"Oh my God!" She leaned forward and kissed him on the cheek then jumped up and down, clapping. "Alright, see ya tomorrow!" She beamed, radiating joy.

"Tomorrow!" he giggled back.

Gator went out the door then immediately stuck his head back in and called, "Hey!"

"*Ahh!*" the girl blurted with a jump. "Oh my God, You scared me!"

"Sorry… What's your name?"

"Katy… Katy Lemonade."

Gator just looked at her.

"Yeah, Katy Lemonade… For real. You can laugh!"

"No. Ya know what…? It's perfect. Twelve – O – one!"

"… *Ooo-Kay*…? Far out."

Free man Roosevelt Delano "Gator" Franklin cakewalked, shoeless, down Railroad Avenue. Things seemed to finally be lining up and, unlike anyone he had ever met, just being in the presence of the persistently positive country hippie, Katy Lemonade, raised his endorphin levels.

It was a good day.

The next few days of work were just mopping and straightening up and restocking the bulk bins and listening to Katy Lemonade be enthused about the smallest things and not getting too granular with the fungibles.

Now it was time to find a house.

A home.

***

JD Hollingsworth

Late May, 1976

"How ya doin' Charlene?"

"Oh, jus' suff'rin' from the mornin' sickness sump'in' awful... Coffee?"

Gator came into Strickland's Diner before work as he always did and now to read the classified ads in the weekly *Utinahicayune* when a peculiar thing happened: a stranger came in.

He parked his big red Riviera on the curb and strolled in like the King of Siam. He was in his sixties, maybe, but tan and fit. He looked like Buster Crabbe and was dressed in that successful-contractor-at-the-country-club style with a pink Lacoste polo shirt, and navy slacks with a white patent leather belt and loafers. He came in chewing an unlit cigar and made known, by proclamation to one and all, that he was one "Hannibal J. Hardcastle of O-hi-yah, Cincinnatah, O-hi-yah" – and as if to allay any doubt of his origins, he worked a pair of large buckeyes around in his fingers.

Not shy on the self-promotion, he went on to point out that everyone surely knew *of* him as he had made a great fortune on television-marketed gadgets. "Certainly, boys certainly," he began with the flair of a carnival huckster, "y'all a-heard a tha kitchen marvel, tha 'Dice-X Machina'..."

"Hey, yeah! I a-hyeard a that!" one of the old men that clogged the corner booth each day piped up.

"Yeah," "Right!" they all agreed.

"'At's right!" Hardcastle crowed, then puffed up and began to strut and ballyhoo, "Friends, ya won't a-get them-a onions diced as nice fer *twice* tha price!"

The old men howled and slapped their knees.

"Whaddaboutha 'Temp-O-Hairy' home adhesive hair plug system," the showman went on, pacing around and pointing at his rapt audience, "...An' tha best-sellin' 'Dog-A-Matic' what a-keeps tha beast a-satisfied without a-havin' ta pay no 'tention..."

His mission now, he boasted, was to develop a great golf resort – one to rival Callaway – and right hereabouts, closer than Callaway to the highway between Atlanta and Florida. He asked about people from the old days who might have property they may "a-needs ta be a-shed of," and showed particular interest in the old Milton Plantation. Hardcastle continued to crow that he always came ready to deal and so was never without "a *big* box a money" and if they would just direct him to the present owners he would "have a parlez an' palaver with 'em that'll a-suit n' a-satisfy all jus' fine, as it-is-always mah aim ta *please*."

Charlene Williams at the register cocked her ear listening, somewhat bedazzled by the bluster, when an awkward young man lurched in the door and slumped to the counter. Gator knew Ansel Bragg from the Rodeway Inn way out on the Vico Road, near the highway, where – no longer able to endure his mother and Skeeve – Gator had been living for the past couple of weeks. Bragg's entrance caused Charlene to chirp up, "Well, glory be, right here, just come in the door's a young feller what's engaged ta... what? A niece? Er cousin? Er somethin' a the Miltons!"

But, to the apparent, and great, disappointment of Hardcastle, young Ansel mumbled without looking up from his menu that Miss Ruby, the last true heir to the property, had only recently passed and that after the Big House was razed, aside from the slave cabins that had been retained by his fiancée's branch for cabins or hunting camps, what land had not already been lost or held in abeyance for a missing beneficiary was sold off to the Georgia-LaRoquefort Corporation for timber and was being logged even as they spoke.

Falling into an odd melancholy now, the puzzling stranger Hardcastle asked if they could at least direct him to the location of the old house as he, for some reason seemingly beyond the mere curiosity of a stranger, wanted to "have a looksee." Told the way, he headed for the door but, spying a quarter on the floor, stopped near the register momentarily. The fat-embolism of old men in the corner booth leaned in expectantly, waiting for the out-of-towner's attempt to pick up the coin, only to be thwarted – they knew – by the epoxy with which they had long ago adhered it to the green linoleum.

Hardcastle looked at the twenty-five cent piece, then to the yearning geriatrics, winked and walked out.

JD Hollingsworth

The geezers leaned disappointedly back into their split vinyl seats with a collective wheeze of actual deflation, and Hannibal J. Hardcastle reclined into the big red Buick and disappeared.

Gator shrugged then reviewed the listings he had circled in the rental notices. The cheapest option, on Mill Spring Lane, past the outskirts of town, seemed the best fit. He stuffed his shirt pocket with the pictures of automobiles and faces and whatnot he had carefully torn from the classifieds and obituaries for his collages and stepped to the diner payphone where he called the number from the listing. A frail and kindly sounding woman on the other end arranged to have him meet a Mr. Anderson the next day and he was filled with hope.

***

The Capri coughed its trail of pale blue exhaust up and down the Fitzgerald Road as Gator drove around and around looking for Mill Spring Lane among the many washboard roads that disappeared deep into the woods and fields along its edge. Finally, he investigated a dirt track he had passed a half dozen times, but not bothered to investigate for, with its entrance almost entirely obscured by splayed foliage buzzing with insects, it hardly seemed like a road at all.

A ways down the dusty path he saw an abandoned trailer's mailbox with "59 Mi l Spr   Ln" pasted there in slanting bronze stickers and knew that he had at least found the road. He crept slowly down the apparently uninhabited trace looking for something that might reveal itself to be a lodgeable structure. At last, at the very end of the road, one abandoned shack sat across the road from two others close together in the shadow of a rusty antique water tower that looked like an old-timey fireworks skyrocket dripping with kudzu. A very much out of place bronze Mercedes Benz 300SEL also sat in that shadow.

Gator pulled over, got out and began to walk towards the vehicle. The big car's door swung open and a large, saggy and unhealthy looking man struggled to climb out of the golden Teutonic sleigh. The man threw his ponderous weight forward several times, finally gaining the momentum required to exit the door and with the aid of a cane he pulled himself unsteadily to his feet. A sloppy bag of man, shaped like an inverted top with Babe Ruth legs wearing khaki pants, a blue shirt, and white suspenders emerged, gasping and sweating. He retrieved from his dashboard, and smashed atop his big head, a straw hat with a transparent green visor in its brim and walked towards Gator with the stiff, side-to-side rocking motion of one of those old ramp-walker toys of Donald Duck or Popeye. As he grew near he began to wipe, or, more accurately, smear, his face with a stained rag and said, "Ya tha... tha" snort huff "Frank..." huff "tha *FRANK*-lin boah?" huff snort – sounding so out-of-breath that Gator feared his bloated fingers were clinging to the crumbling edge of his last moments of life.

"Yes sir..."

huff snort "Well... well, ah been a" huff "a-*wait*in' heah fuh fie, six *minute!*" snort

His tongue slurped and licked in constant motion like a monitor lizard.

"I'm sorry... sir. It was... difficult ta find." Gator said with forced cordiality.

"Hahd ta *FAHND*!?" snort slurp "Damn hell boah!" huff "S'raht heyah!" snort. "Whu'd ya'a... a damn... *ID-yut?*" smack

Gator felt the anger chemicals seeping into his blood stream. "Okay!.... O...Kay..." He took a deep breath. "Alright... Stay calm," he thought to himself, then acquiesced aloud, "Okay, sorry... Is-the-place-still-for-rent?"

"*Still fuh RENT?*" smack "Ah..." huff "Ah only been heyah fuh... fuh three, fo *minute...*" slurp snort "Hell you say, 'still fuh rent'... Who th'... Who *tha fuck* I s'pose ta ren' it tuh in three minute?"

Gator stood, squinting hard, sighed, then, in a too measured tone, asked, "May-I-See-It?"

huff "*Whooooooo hooo*" slurp "Well... Ya... Ya suhtanly *mmmay...* Nancy." snort

Gator followed John Anderson into the house nearest the road, just next to the abandoned and overgrown one beneath the tower. It was the usual crap old rental house found in small Southern towns. It had once been a Spartan but cozy craftsman-style mill house, but over the past five decades old window frames had become funhouse parallelograms, their deviations from the right filled with pounds of indiscriminately injected caulk; Weldwood paneling had been slapped up, then half of it removed, and what was left was held on with duct tape at its edges; a partial and poorly installed suspended acoustic-tile ceiling checkerboarded overhead and what tiles remained were stained with abstract art motifs in various hues of amber.

"That... that space heatuh theyah... say it's" snort "*DANE*-j'rus..." huff grunt "So don'... don' be a... be a-SLAY-pin' wi' it own." hack

On the collapsing enclosed back porch of delaminating plywood was an old Kenmore dryer that housed a possum family, the stove in the kitchen had never had the spaghetti sauce splatters chiseled off and the phone-booth-like plastic shower stall that had replaced the old iron tub (removed to the back yard for mosquito breeding purposes) may have once been white beneath the greenish-black mold, but was now the color of cream corn.

The unfiltered aroma of failure larded the otherwise stale air.

huff "this a goo... a good damn house heyah. Ya too dumb not ta take it, some" huff slurp "some othuh froot come snatch it up raht quick!" smack snort

"Let me look aroun' a little more..."

"Look *'roun'*? Whus they ta" huff "ta see? Ain't got awl day..." hack huff "'nuthuh boah a-comin' ta look... ya bettah sign this heyah lease..." huff slurp "Know whas' good fuh yah." honnk

Gator felt the rage and said he was going out to look at the yard, just to get some distance between himself and the sour old wheezing bagpipe of phlegm.

"The *yahd?* Yah bettah...b-"

The door closed behind Gator and he walked down the front steps, out into the unkempt but living heath.

He dwelled there for a while among the knee-high brush and bramble in the hot sun regaining his composure, feeling, moment-by-moment, reassured by the unguided gardens, the junky floridness of this land that here so quickly overtakes the ignored places, and became calm once more. All around, the grass, the trees, the flowers, the weeds – if here there was distinction – were not just alive but teemed with life within: the air filled with the "click *zzzzzzzz* click *zzzzzzz* click *zzzzzzz*..." transmissions of the insect telegraph; a brown thrasher improvised a scat tune from some high and hidden place; Red Admiral and orbiting pairs of Sulfur butterflies danced about its woven greenery and flowerings; a single cicada, whose call having yet months of merriness before falling to the long and mournful cry of late summer, chattered away in a Chinaberry tree which, with its clouds of lilac flowers teeming in honeybees, provided the field's only shade beyond that of the rusting, kudzu-draped tower.

His senses sharpened to all things. In the heat he became keenly aware of the drop of sweat that weaved its way down his forehead then crept along the bridge of his nose to the end where it hung to infinitesimally vibrate with expectancy of the fall, and the sensation galvanized his mind, shot a rush of excitement through him like a thunderbolt: ecstasy at the intense perception of this simple thing. Then he drew a quick breath and turned with an uncanny sense of another presence.

He took notice of the overgrown and un-pruned mass of thorny vines, heavy with fat heirloom roses, veiling the porch of the abandoned house next door, which he now saw hung upon the edge of a gully and its shimmering pool weeping from the rock from which, he guessed, this eponymous glorified cattle path took its name. But there was... something else.

He turned back for a moment as Anderson, cigarette in hand and soaking with sweat, struggled, one slow step at a time, down the stairs to the yard, slobbering and gasping like a ruptured bellows with every half-inch of progress.

"Ya... ya" huff snort slurp "well... ya wan'tha damn house uh not?"

Gator slowly turned away from the heaving mass of edema to look back upon the old grandmother's garden fantasia next door, sensing *something*.

"I.... I..." he stuttered and felt dizzy.

"Needs ta... Needs ta sign this heyah... this heyah LEASE!"

Gator felt his senses – focused entirely upon the entwined, flowing host of blossoms – sharpen again, but could still only lethargically voice, "I..."

The air was still, there was no wind, yet the florid tangle obscuring the porch steps seemed to move, to swell: to take a breath.

"I..."

And, it spoke.

The flowing mass of roses, boasted, "I sees you, but ya cain't see me! ... heeheeheeheeheeheehee..."

" ...*What?*"

"Said... I sees *you*, but ya cain't see me!" the plant repeated.

Gator stood, hypnotized. "You... *can*...?"

Then, as if from a mist, an old woman, not five feet tall, emerged from the mass of blossoms, vines and stalks. She stepped forth from the jungle like Henry Stanley, drifted over with a toothless smile, and took hold to Gator's arm. The multiple, colorful calico housedresses she wore, one upon the other, and the gingham apron above it all bestowed upon her the psychedelic regalness of a Celestial Empress Dowager, and had perfectly camouflaged her, like some tropical mantis hiding in plain sight on the jungle orchid it mimics, among the crazy quilt of untamed inflorescence from which she had materialized. A mass of intricately braided gray hair crowned her head. A dribble of dried snuff juice streaked her chin. She smelled like a hobo.

"I bet you a-thought them roses was *a-talkin'* ta ya, heeheeheehee"

He felt dizzy again and mumbled, "I... I *diiid,*" like a sleepy child.

snort "Boah! Ya wan' it, uh not?" huff slurp

"I..."

Even Anderson's grotesque, mucilaginous honking could not break the spell of her enchantment.

"I..."

The drop fell from Gator's nose and the garden empress began to sing,

> *With plen'y a water an' plen'y a oil*
> *An' the best gas that mo-ney can buyyy,*
> *On a dan-ger-ous curve*
> *Ac-ci-dents will occur,*
> *So why DON'T ya let JE-sus take a-hold a the wheel*
> *An' y'll make it*
> *Ta Heaven*
> *On High*

"Yeah, I *want* this house."

***

May 31, 1976

peep peep peep   deedle deedle deedle   peep peep peep
peep peep peep   deedle deedle deedle   peep peep peep

Some tiny songbird chirping from the old woman's Chinaberry tree awoke Gator. He rubbed his eyes, looked up from the floor, and chuckled, "Oh, man... that's... adorable."

He was raised the woods and loved nature and animals and hunting and after the years in lockup to hear this simple repetitive tune, with all of the complexity and timbre of a child playing upon a toy piano, brought him ever so slightly back to life. He inhaled suddenly and deeply to feel that life rush into him. Then, just as suddenly, he stopped and held it. It all filled his heart with joy, and he tensed his stomach to contain a tiny laugh that danced within him, as if his ribs caged a flittering, chirping bird of their own. He could have lain there for hours, but he had to get up and mop the floors at the store.

But, then, that girl was there too. That Katy Lemonade. And she was easy on the eyes. He couldn't even let himself think of how that compared to prison. But now, a home of his own, a job... and so on, he felt almost like one of those folks that lived in the brick ranchers out on the roads with two ditches.

peep peep peep   deedle deedle deedle   peep peep peep

***

June 25, 1976

"Alright, here's some stuff, prob'ly help ya out," Gator said, dropping two brown paper bags on the tiny counter behind the television, whose position between Arlene and Skeeve on the couch and himself presented the illusion that they were paying attention to him.

They were not.

"Yeah, some burger... Uhh... Looked like ya was outta mayonnaise last I looked... so there's some Duke's. The good stuff..." All he heard in return was Johnny Olson yelling about a waterbed from the television.

Gator stood for a moment, then lit a Camel and pulled back the edge of a bag with his finger to look in. "Oh, yeah... some Pringles... I know ya like the Pringles..." and he looked hopefully back to the fossilized couple. Johnny Olson yelled about a 25-inch color TV and a record changer.

He stood in the kitchenette just holding the cigarette to his lips and watching the dead eyes of his mother and Skeeve.

"Bacon..." he went on after a minute.

"Luncheon loaf..."

"Vienna sausages..."

"Streak o' lean ..."

Olson yelled about a four-cylinder Ford Mustang with a vinyl roof.

"Yeah... an' some vegetables too," Gator called loudly, "Need ta eat your *vegetables!*" Approving applause floated by from the television.

He called out, "... Chicken greens... Hog sprouts... Vine-ripened goat ass..." like a military roll call, then waited much too long for any kind of response. There was none. He looked at his watch then ran his cigarette under the tap and left the butt in the sink.

Bob Barker said, "The actual retail price of your showcase is..."

"*Two thousand five hundred dollars!*" Gator quickly intervened.

Skeeve and Arlene both shot angry glances at Gator that immediately returned to the television.

Gator turned and pushed open the trailer door saying, "Well, don't wanna *fuck up* your showdown," as he hit the steps.

"Toooo laaate..." Skeeve drawled from behind like Huckleberry Hound.

Gator stood for moment then loped down the last few steps and jumped into the Capri saying, "Got shit ta do," under his breath, and disappeared down the driveway and out of the park.

As Gator returned to the main road from his detour down to Rangle's Branch for one of the things he had to do on his way back to work, he hefted the baggie of plant matter in his right hand and groaned that it appeared to be almost all stems. He looked back to the road just in time to notice, and swerve to avoid, a person along the side of the road. In his rear view mirror he could see it was his mysterious neighbor in the "abandoned" house – Marie – shuffling along with her walking stick. Almost immediately after he had identified her she turned from the narrow shoulder and down the embankment into the woods.

"Well, that's... kinda fuckin' weird," he said, and continued glancing back and forth from the road ahead to the mirror until the point of her disappearance into the woods itself disappeared in the distance. He thought of how he had no idea what went on with her: here, or back home by the spring. He thought no one knew what happens back there.

Immediately upon entering the Health Hole Gator found himself being questioned by a sad Katy Lemonade: how was he today, and he said, "great;" were all guys jerks, he said that they were; "why," she wondered, he said they just were; was he was a jerk, and he was called to the back office. There, Poshlost worked to reattach the shelf unit that had fallen off the wall again in the night and Gator assumed he was being called in to take over the task.

"*Que pasa*, bossman," he said with a sort of lazy enthusiasm on entering the back room, hoping to initiate a more relaxed, human, interaction.

But Poshlost began his workspeak, "So... Ga-... I... I don't want to call you *'Gator'*... But, what...? Roosevelt, Rosey... Delano... Del... I don't know what... how to..."

"How 'bout 'Gator'?"

"I'm in a hurry so, yes, for now... Anyway... *Ga-tor*... smaller minds may wish to continue to get by, only grasping for the low-hanging fruit, but I think to more fully, holistically, integrate you into the larger oeuvre we were hoping to more fully actualize – to exploit, if you will – your intellectual capital within the point-of-sale community, seeing as that is a major component of our income-driving sector, and we have, of late, suffered the loss of our leading exponent on the floor..."

"Brother, you must be *hell* in Scrabble," Gator plauded.

"I don't play *Scra-bulll*..." Poshlost groaned with disdain.

"Yeah... me neither. Gave it up... Had a bad experience..."

"No. And I would have hoped that you've become aware of it by this point, but... I try to surround myself with only... only the *finer* things..."

"*Scrabble's* fine!" Gator shot back with genuine indignation.

"It's not one of the better games... Certainly not one of the *best*," the disheveled manager went on with misplaced arrogance. "I choose only Milton Bradley games. Milton Bradley makes the best games in the world."

"*Ha!* That's... wait. You're kiddin'..."

"Do I seem funny?"

Gator considered his answer carefully. On the one hand...

"No, sir..." was the path he, perhaps wisely, chose. "So... no Scrabble. Or Monopoly..."

"No, but..."

"Jus'... Chutes an' Ladders an'... Mystery Date."

"I..."

"Kreskin's ESP..."

"I think this conversation has gotten a little off the rails... I'd like to continue..."

"Okay, shoot."

"To..."

"... an' ladder."

"… …'huff…" Poshlost paused ominously for a moment, then remembered Gator had been in prison, and continued. "To make a teeee-diously *long* conversation short, we recently lost our vitamin and supplement customer service representative and need someone to be out there interacting with our very active remedy and nutritional enhancement base."

"You want me ta be the *vitamin guy?*"

Poshlost groaned, "In a word, 'yes.'"

"Replace the *orange* guy?"

"Yes. And yes, he drank a great deal of carrot juice."

"You know I don't know *anything* 'bout it."

"Our customers are very… self-informed. Just reassure them and sell them what they want."

"*Oohhhh*-kay."

"Now I have things to do."

"Alright." Gator walked out, calling back, "Anchors… sheetrock…"

"*Thank* yoooo."

He walked to the counter where Katy was reading.

"Hi," he greeted.

"OH! Hi! How are you!?" she gasped with joy, as if she had not seen Gator in years.

"Doin' great. Just like three minutes ago."

"What happened three minutes ago?" she asked, wide-eyed, as if being let in on a secret.

"I mean… doin' great, just like I was… three minutes ago…"

"That's so cool."

"Yeah, it is. How are you?"

"Okay… I guess," she sighed, still sad and running her finger across the cover of a book on the counter. Then, energized, she piped, "Oh! Reading *the* scariest thing *ever* from the book section."

Gator turned his head upside down to see the cover. "Robert Anton Wilson… Yeah, I think that's… supposed ta… be a joke."

"Oh… Do you read?"

"Yeah, I read."

"What's your favorite book."

"Ehhhhh…" he mused, seemingly put out. "I don't know. *Moby Dick?*"

"I read that… in school!" Katy effused. "Why do you think it's so great?"

"Hmmm, well, it manages ta address everything in the human condition without ever leavin' a boat… So, there's that… I guess. You read *Moby Dick?*"

"Yeah... well, except for all the stuff 'bout whales. But this book is scary!"

"The one that's a joke?"

"Yeahhhhhhh."

"Anyways, I'm the new vitamin guy!" Gator said, changing the subject.

"No-freaking-way! That is *soooo* far out! Do you know 'bout all that?"

"Not a thing!" he chirped.

"I do!... if you want help, I'll study with you!"

"Alright!"

"That would be *soooo* cool!"

"It will!"

The 441 White Line Fevers were playing that night and Gator felt good so he stayed from happy hour to well into their set. They were really not half bad, he thought, and he was genuinely enjoying them mix it up, going from "Good Hearted Woman" to "Tumbling Dice" and even to Red Sovine's new hit, "Teddy Bear." The beer, which he was now permitted to consume, was cold, that same little sausage was riding up and down in the big pickle jar, and Katy was going to teach Gator about homeopathy, whatever that was... and "(Don't Take Her) She's All I Got" just started playing.

"Paycheck!" Gator bellowed. "*Fuuuck* yeah! Whooooo!"

"*Paycheck... Fuck yeah....*" came from behind him in a low, mocking voice, "Hahaha!"

He turned around to see Katy Lemonade standing close behind him with a beer.

"Goofball... Didn't think *you* got excited 'bout *any*thing."

"Sssorry..." Gator slurred, and hung his head.

"Don't apologize!"

She was right. There were so many things about readjusting to life on the outside: the light switch; that a normal bed was too comfortable to actually sleep on now; that it was always time to eat whenever "chow time" hours came around, even if he wasn't hungry, even if he didn't know what time it was. Even if he didn't know what time it was, he still knew what time it was in prison. And now, he realized, that he had lost certain abilities: the ability to socialize, in a normal way; to not keep self-erected walls around himself; to not view every interaction with suspicion. Everyone in prison was preying upon or playing everyone else. It was the way it was. Finding the correct way to interact now was difficult. Added to this, that he was drunk and had always been awkward, shy, around women, he had returned to the social skills and confidence of the acne-pocked fourteen year-old of twelve years ago. He felt suddenly dumb and struggled for something to talk about.

He slurred, "Man... that pedal sssteel player... he'sss... he's pretty good, but man, he is so... *int... intense.*"

"Yeah, I guess... You know that's his wife comes in the store all the time? ...The Seventh-day Adventist."

"Really? With the... the yella kids that ahhlwa... always have the sniffles... an'... red eyesss?"

"Yeah. You'll get to know her... she buys *a lllot* of medicine."

"Me-di-cine..." Gator said, squinting circumspectly, "*Yeahhhhh... Hey!* How'd'ju end up here..? Or there...? The sstore..."

"Poshlost," she simply replied.

"Yeah, with Puhh... Poshhlossst."

"That's what I mean... *with* Todd."

"*What?*"

"I came here with Todd. Met at Byron and... I don't know. Just ended up back here."

"You're *with... Poshlosst?*" Gator gasped, aghast.

"Not any more. But then... for a while... yeah." Katy fell silent then mused, "Gosh, that was a million light years ago..."

"Sssooo, that'ss, like... ssseven million dog light yearsss..." Gator said, choosing to ignore the metrics error.

"Hmmmpf!" She snapped with as much frustrated bad temper as she was capable. "Are you ever serious?"

"Thought I was al... alwa... alwayss seriouss," he said, realizing he just didn't know what to say anymore.

"I have terrible taste in men..." Katy went on. "But it worked out, ya know? I mean, I am *so* happy to be here and working at the store and learning things and it's nice around here... in a *totally* weird way... And now I know you," and she smiled. "I don't know... guess you have to go through... uncool things to get to cooler ones."

Gator raised his eyebrows, nodded and slurred in knowing agreement, "Frank... Frannnkenssein... *Frank*-en-*STEIN*'s Paradox."

"What!?"

"Dealin' through ssomethin' ya... ahhh... ahhh... ya fear, or hate... or what's ant... ant... an-ti-*thet*-i-cal ta... ta one's na-ture... ta get ta sssomethin' better... sssomethin' whass's good... through somethin' ba... bad... Fffrankenssein's Paradox," and he poked out his lower lip and nodded with authority.

"Why is that Fran-... "

Gator scrunched up into his "explaining face," held his hands up to gesticulate and attempted lucidity. "See... Fruh... Frankenssein... he hated fire... *Haaaated*... Evr'wuh... Ever'one know knows that... Fire... Hated... but he... ahhh... he liked a guh... a good ssmssmoke... Cigar, see?. But... you can't *have* a sm... a ssmoke without a light... fire... ya see? *Sssso* he dealt... with with the fire an' he... he got him a sm a ssmoke... Fire bad... ssm smoke goood... or... or... ya know, like you sssa sssaid, go through uncool thi thingss ta get what a cooler oness... See? ...Frankensssein's Paradox."

"You are *so* funny! I love you. But you better get on home. Are you okay, man? Can you *drive?*"

"I'll... I'll walk."

"That's, like... *a mile.*"

He put his hand around the back of her neck and said, "Ffflower child... d'ya know wha... what it'ss like ta not ta not ta be able ta walk *noooo*where? Ever? *Ehhh*-ver? ahhh... An' then... an' then... be able ta..." he dropped to a whisper, "an' an' then be ta able ta walk *ANNNNY* where ya ya want? As farrr as as wu as ya want? ..." He teared up. "... Ss'beeyootiful."

He smiled and planted a kiss on her nose and she snorted.

"Twelve – *Ooooh* – one..." He announced.

"...*O-Kay*...? ... What does that *mean?*"

"Meanss... ..." Gator looked away, puckered his lips and inhaled deeply through his nose and said, "... Re-*lease*..." with a quick nod.

He wandered out of Miss Her waving back over his head and she laughed again.

Gator walked and walked and walked singing,
"*Ahhh'm beggin' ya fre-uh-end,*
Don' take 'er, she's awll I gawwwt
She's ehhh-v'rythaaang in life ah'll ever nee-uh-eed..."
the whole way home.

He climbed the stairs to his creaking screen door where he leaned against the wall to regain his balance and smile. The tangled vines over on Marie's porch sparkled like Christmas from the scores of lightning bugs drawn there and within their frame he saw the orange glow from Marie's pipe. It grew brighter from a draw and Gator faintly saw her grinning face. It disappeared in a pale blossom of Prince Albert and he heard, "Night be coooool."

"*Hahaha*, darn tootin', Marie... An' so are you!" he called back.

Joyous cackling came from among the flashing beetles and Gator stumbled inside where, with his face pressed to the paneling and his knees nearly buckled, he leaned against the wall and flipped his light on and off for half an hour to the music in his head. He thought there might, at last, be something good on the other side of all of this awfulness.

He stumbled back outside to ask the night if Katy had said she loved him.

The bugs in the trees agreed that Katy did, and he staggered back inside where he dropped to the floor and upon a bed of colorful paper clippings he lay down with a pillow cool as a cat's ear and slept.

***

III

JD Hollingsworth

August 1, 1976

"Rent *TAHHHHM!*"

As predictable as the months themselves, and on the first of each, Anderson appeared, and always at dawn, in Gator's front yard yelling, "Rent tahhhm! Rent tahhhm!" snort.

Gator awoke with a start, for a moment thinking he was still in prison, then shook his head and looked out the window to see Anderson shuffling toward the house with his cane.

huff smack "Rent tahhhm!" huff

Gator climbed off the meditation pad on the floor grumbling and profanely invoking the King of Kings. He grabbed his pants, draped across the space heater, pulled the sixty-five dollars he had ready from the pocket and walked out onto the porch. Here, Gator noted – as he would come to know as usual on the monthly affirmation of John Anderson's property ownership – that Anderson was urinating on the front steps from the ragged yard.

He looked up from his penis to Gator coming out the screen door in his boxers.

snort "Yah... y'otta" huff "Y'otta put own sum" huff "own sum *TROU*-zuhs 'fo' ya comes t'th'doah'!"

"Yeah, can I jus' bring the rent ta *you* on the first?"

"No suh, yah suhtanly can *not*," Anderson retorted as he began up the four stairs to meet Gator's cash, his penis still dangling. "Ah needs ta come 'spect" huff snort "'spect mah *PRAH*-puh-ty. Check *up* own it," and he banged on the half-torn out door screen with his cane.

"...Okay, well, in that case, could ya have Darnell fix that leak under the sink... again?" Gator grumbled.

huff "Whu'? It still a" smack huff "still a-*LAY*-kin'?" snort

"Obviously... Okay, I need ta get ready for work."

"'At's raht. Ya does." huff "Rent tahm come ehhh'vrah muunth."

"Don't I know it..."

Strickland's was all abuzz with talk of the find up out on the highway.

Boys chasing an armadillo had discovered the stranger's red Riviera, exposed in the still smoking aftermath of a controlled burn, in the woods not far off of the road out near the old Milton place. The state police would later report that it was registered to a Chester O. Fish of 13 Detroiter Ave, Elsea Mobile Village, Winesburg, Ohio, and that neither could he be located nor was any trace nor record of Hannibal J. Hardcastle to be found: in fact, of *any* Hannibal J. Hardcastle. Anywhere. Ever. Aside from the Riviera, all that was found was a rifled suitcase and a box of magazines and old comic books from decades ago dumped on the side of the road near where the big red automobile had been rolled into the briars.

The box and its contents were thrown away and the Buick impounded.

Charlene Williams leaned in. "I heard..." she said, looking away and back again, then under her breath disclosed, "they seen The *Ape* out there, 'roun' then..."

Gator knew of "The Ape." Everyone in Utinahica knew of The Ape. The Ape, or "the Spring Valley Ape," as he was more formally addressed for that part of the town outskirts he was known to haunt, was, like Old Smudgee and the Ghost Child of Paradise, a shade of local legend – but a more powerful, pervasive presence: a mythical (or not) creature that roamed the countryside and was considered not a mere cryptozoological, Sasquatch-type beast, but, like a lone crow on a fencepost, a harbinger of doom. Late night motorists sometimes saw him, fleetingly, in moonlit fields or woodland borders, howling and raving, or glimpsed his distinctive gait crossing the road at the edge of the headlights' distant throw. On occasion his presence was betrayed in the shadows of the forest by his trademarked glowing green eyes.

Marie, next door, had said that she herself, "a-know'd 'im by name," but Gator didn't know if that meant she had only heard of it being mentioned, or, just as likely, that she was on a first-name basis with the thing.

Real or imagined, his legend went back years and almost every Utinahican could remember his many famous appearances around the time of strange or tragic incidents such as trailer fires, those murders and unexplained disappearances, like young "Lucky" Anderson and that horrible mess left behind. There was also the Decoration Day Okgatalatchee Bridge collapse, when scores of Ape sightings were reported just before and after that engineering failure had taken three known lives and left one child never to be found in the river. There were also, in the day, tales told of his presence during the unpleasantness of '59. The *dilettante* Ape enthusiast would say that that nightmarish occurrence, the vision leading to it, and its aftermath were the origin of The Ape, but those with ears long to the ground knew it to be much, much older. In fact, before revolutionary zeal prevented him from fraternizing with The Man, Gator's prisonmate, Jericho Milton, had told Gator that he knew of The Ape well before "The Incident" in 1959, for the specter had been used far back into the misty generations of his community as a "boogerman" to frighten and correct the willful child. He himself had been warned countless times, "You bette' *git* in'is house right *now* an' stop a *lolly*gaggin' outside or th'*Ape* a-come an' *haul* you 'way!!!" In fact, as far as those in his community knew – a community with long and deep ties to the native inhabitants – the story went far back into "Indian times" and the Ape could well have been related to the wandering Wog of Nodoroc.

No less than *Fate* magazine had even reported of the Ape's association with the great Georgia UFO wave of 1973. Between the ads for the Rosicrucians and the Prophecies of Nostradamus, in the *True Mystic Experiences* miscellany ("Competent Reporting On Unusual Topics") there was this:

Frankenstein's Paradox

"I Battled A Gorilla From Outer Space!"
by the Reverend Collier D. Pine

The night was not unlike any other as I motored along our quaint byway, the Fitzgerald Road, yet, somehow, though having just comforted my flock with an evening's sermon on the Lord's ever watchful and protective presence, I felt a sense of trepidation. Suddenly, above the treetops of the forest I knew so well and in the heavens from which I found solace, there came a vision: a vision which struck terror into my very heart! A glowing object surrounded by flashing lights appeared and hovered, only to then drop with frightening suddenness onto the road ahead of my speeding automobile! *"Was this one of the mysterious aerial craft of which we have heard so much of late?"* I asked myself. Now, as I sat helpless in the ditch and regaining my senses following the impact upon leaving the road, the pulsing disk released several of its *saucermen* who approached with arms outstretched! Knowing that my survival, my very fate upon this World, was in my hands and my hands alone, I retrieved the .44 from the glove box to blast away at the *silver-suited UFOnauts*, forcing their retreat back to the rarefied regions. But neither my safety, nor that of Earth, was yet assured! Little did I know that I was still not out of danger until attempting to deliver my high-centered Cadillac from the gully. For then, a giant ape, or *ape-like creature* from beyond, emerged from the forest and came fiercely upon me, wailing its inhuman wail, which can never be sponged from my memory! Certain that the unholy beast had been left behind as a soldier in the Martian's pre-invasion shock troops, I reloaded and emptied my weapon at the thing! Whether I struck the horror or not I shall never know, but as it fled back into its woodland haunts, I knew that though I had walked through the valley of the shadow, that for then, *for now*, and by the grace and protection of Smith & Wesson and our *Lord Jesus Christ*, we were safe.

Terrifying times indeed.
Now though, for reasons known only to The Ape, his base was within the old warehouses and silos of the long-abandoned factory and

grain storage district known as "the Mills," in Spring Valley: near the location of the Reverend Pine's encounter, and within sight of Gator's home. Gator had noted, with his usual drollness, that – aside from being used to make ordinary tragedies seem more significant or as celebrity fiend in fireside haint tales – these days, and in keeping with his role as omen of unpleasant things to come, the Ape was now used mostly by teenagers – parked among the old brick buildings or those brave enough to venture within, flashlight in hand – for premature orgasms, noting that fear, for some reason, was conducive to painfully brief high school sex and was, sadly for The Ape's legacy, the origin of most of his sightings these days.

More scientifically, therefore finally, a local amateur anthropologist had, by this time, been documenting Ape sightings and collecting physical evidence, such as it was, for years. Perhaps because of the dense pine-needle carpet of the local forest floor and the hard red clay beneath, the Spring Valley Ape just did not deliver regarding the giant footprint evidence so relished by Sasquatologists. Physical evidence was, in general, rare: broken branches; a few stray hairs. It was, however, a veritable bonanza when it came to spoor. Stools, identified by the anthropologist to be clearly not of any normal forest inhabitant, had been collected, desiccated, and boxed – labeled with provenancial data and cross-referenced with a pin-studded map of Georgia – then stored away in the anthropologist's ever-expanding bank of flat files. The map, with pins color-coded for sightings, encounters, physical evidence and even the one short tape-recording of his distant, hair-raising yowl, presented no doubt that Spring Valley was indeed the statistical and geographic center of Ape activity, though one pin impaled the map as far away as Ludowici.

One of the coin-gluers in the corner booth who resembled a weathered board with a nail through it leaning against the sun-faded leatherette, spoke up and loudly indicated that everyone was stupid. Old Man Duquesne, the prison twin's father and the ultimate possessor of the stranger's red Buick via sheriff's auction postured, "'Spesh'ly anybody what done bought *that* hog..." warping the long gray plank of his body back as if to adopt a proud bearing.

"Ah'd a hafta been four days on a corn jug ta b'lieve *that* pig shit."

Strangely, for that group, the old coot seemed the very voice of reason and he opined with self-aware majesty that the world was full of murder and mayhem, and that it was all "jus' assholes a-doin' shit."

Frankenstein's Paradox

***

On his way to the Health Hole Gator encountered some children giving away a box of kittens. Gator picked up a skinny black one with green eyes, and gave him one of "those" cat names on the spot. He brought him into the store – to Katy Lemonade's joy and to Todd Poshlost's condemnation: with health codes and there being "foodstuffs on the premises," and whatnot.

Not wanting to get too personal or open with anyone, much less Poshlost, Gator still felt need to explain that, after more than three years in lockdown, he had found in freedom many pitfalls. One was an attenuated ability to interact, to relate appropriately, to others and he felt that an animal, a pet, would help him to socialize and, frankly, that it would be the first trustworthy friend he had had in years. In his heart of hearts Gator may also have felt a desire to have another being over which he could exercise control, dominion, whose freedom he might regulate, but in choosing a cat he had, of course, made a mistake.

He went on that he understood Poshlost's position and certainly did not wish to jeopardize his job, but hoped he would allow it just through this day: lying, in a grandiose coda, that he felt Todd to be a wise and just man. Todd sighed and began to speak, which always tended to make Gator's mind wander: as it did now. But this time, as he drifted off – the limp black cat hanging indifferently from his hand – his gaze wandered as well and he saw on the street outside, Marie. There she was, right outside his window, with a black plastic bag on her head for a sort of do-rag, and shaking the old potato dibbler she used as a cane at Everett Lawson – just walking down the street on break from the feed mill and minding his own business. Poshlost's voice faded to faint, insect-like buzz and Gator cocked his head to one side like a confused dog. He squinted to wonder upon how it was that he had never known of, nor even *seen*, Marie before he moved out by the spring. Now there she was, again, out in the world, like that time out on the road, and now just mere yards from where he stood, from where he worked, haranguing someone on a downtown street, right outside his window. She was an oddball; certainly he would have noticed her before in the years he had lived in Utinahica.

Gator wondered what bizarre tale or fact, like those he had come to know well, she was transmitting to Lawson – though he seemed less interested or amused than would have Gator under the same circumstances. As Gator wondered, he heard Poshlost groan and snapped back to paying attention to his monologue as his job might well depend upon its outcome. Poshlost, unaware of Gator's absence, droned on, pointing out,

"I have many, *many* problems of my own – petty annoyances each and every day – and I believe there to be scarce few who could even begin to fathom their complexity or meaning at more than a back-of-the-envelope level, much less care... care to the extent that it would move *them* to make accommodation for my... ughhh... Thank God I'm a lawyer. But, just to counsel you on your issues, a view from a higher level... not just from the astute businessman you know me to be but... as a *more* perspicacious observer... I will share my wisdom and impart to you this: there are more important things in life than a job... and lucre, and I think freedom – cor-po-re-al... from the physical plane perspective – is overrated. True freedom lies within... Perhaps your time... ahem... a-way... might have been better spent seeking a... a higher plane."

Poshlost's smarmily drooled philosophy may have been truth. It may have been correct, accurate, righteous, but it was also pointless, self-serving and most of all, annoying – like when customers in the store explained where meat came from. This smack across the face with a cold, dead fish of dismissiveness, pulled from the shallow waters of condescension, began to make Gator's internal brain communications go all Babel and was quickly eliminating any prefrontal extinction of his aggression response. He really wanted to hit Poshlost – hard, and in the face – and his brain's moral judge was absent from the bench to issue a restraining order: only the dangling cat in his hand kept it from forming a fist and a blow. His pulse-rate quickened as his rage grew and he clenched his free fist and there was gnashing of teeth.

Poshlost mused once more that, "Life itself is nothing, it has no meaning... it is all just preliminaries. Even the race itself is training... If you are unfulfilled, this too shall pass... Better luck next time... all that..."

Gator was trembling, sizzling like a Roman candle about to blow. Poshlost lifted his own lazy lids to see Gator's eyes clenched, his mouth stretched tight in a rictus of containment, which Poshlost mistook only as artifacts of sadness and pain.

"Oh dear..." he sighed. "We all die... Shall I mourn for you now?"

Gator's eyes popped open, bulging with fury. Ready to strike, his now hyper-intense focus fell upon the carefully stacked tower of fallen books and the little heap of drywall dust that had been swept into a perfectly square pile by the baseboard that lay directly before him. The neatly bundled shelf hardware, the – now fifty-four – blown out screw holes in the sheetrock, the shelves themselves, leaning against the wall awaiting their next shot, all forced their way up his optic nerve and exploded inside his brain into a white void like that which had swallowed the chow hall clock in prison and then a calmness began to flow into his bloodstream like some warm and comforting homemade broth.

The white cloud dissipated and he saw the drill and the half-empty box of screws that Poshlost was about to use to make future ruined holes fifty-five through sixty-three, and he felt as though he were rising off the ground and filled with a perfect emotional equilibrium.

The trap had snapped not to havoc, but satori.

Just in the nick of time, there had, at long last, come the dearly-sought coping device: Todd Poshlost's pathetic attempts to hang a set of shelves, and his failure, time and again. Better than the meditation, or the laborious collages, the schadenfreude of Todd's *repetition* compulsion, his living embodiment of the willful ignorance of Santayana's maxim, provided release from Gator's torment, was the soothing tonic the brain squeezin's misappropriations in Gator's aggression-related neural circuits thirsted for.

"Thanks, Siddhartha!" Gator chirped with a cheery zest.

"… You're *wel*-come?"

Gator floated six inches off the ground into the front of the store. He glided with the limp cat still resignedly along for the ride through the natural remedies section where the wife of the 441 White Line Fever's pedal steel guitar man roamed. As an Adventist and a strict believer that it was a sin to intervene in God's plan and seek *medical* attention, she was, as always, every day, there for some unguent or embrocation, some extract or specific or dilution, root or brew to intervene in the apparently perpetual malaise and low-level respiratory distress her family seemed to suffer. What would it be today? He was only too happy to help.

Belladonna? Gelsemium? Pulsatilla? Elderberry Syrup?

Just some good old echinacea?

Today it was Mercurius Solubilis 30 C and Arsenicum Album 30X globules.

Gator looked down to the yellow, sniffling children and piped, "Good luck!" then the mother asked "Wha's th' bes' thing ya got fer… *male i*-ssues?"

He assumed she meant poor tumescence and directed her to the yohimbe bark, herbal stay-hard cream, and the shiny metallic pills from Germany but with African huts on the box that the he called "silver bullets." Though, if the customer who had come into the store time and again mumbling about a need for "enuhjee," while flexing his forearm up from his crotch, and his large and angry wife, standing behind him, arms folded, eyes burning holes through Gator in a fierce and needy glare that screamed, "Mm *hmmm*. You *bettah* come up wi' *sump'in'*!" were to be believed, not a one of these worked. In fact, in an effort to verify the claims of the many supplements sold in the Health Hole, Gator had subjected himself to most of the establishment's stock of treatments and remedies. The bullets – for him, at least – had produced the opposite of the desired effect, giving him only the undesirable physical side-effects of the "Mr. Natural" blotter acid he had done in Reidsville, and had not only not supplied any of LSD's transcendent insight or mystical journeys, they had also reduced his manhood to a tiny button.

Gator got better, but now, upon perusing the enhancement selection, the young mother replied, "No, I mean, male *i*-ssues... like prostrates an'... *tes*-tuh-ckles."

"Uh... yeah... uhhhh, I-think-that-that-is... uh puhhhhh-puh-puh-puh... puh-*lantain?*" and he picked up a bottle of Gaia's Goodness brand "Plantain Power."

"I thinks ya means palmetto... saw palmetto," she corrected.

"Oh, yeah. Right, right... yeah..." he agreed, pointed up and down the shelf, "uhhh...let's see... buh-buh-buhbuh-buh... *Ah!* Here ya go! Saw palmetto! 'Palmetto Power,' 150 mg. That sounds... strong."

"I thinks this hyear is fer... reg'lar maint'nance. I – well, muh husban' – need somethin' a little more... *extry* strenth. I mean, what'd ya recammen' fer a man what's *tes*-tuh-ckles done swole up the size a grapefruits? An' I means *each* a one..."

Gator dropped those six inches back to the floor pretty quickly. He dropped the cat, and, when the voice inside his head stopped screaming at the picture that had popped up in there, he advised, "I-would-recommend-goin'-ta-the-doctor... like, *right – now...* "

"NO. We don' go no doctur. It's all jes' a 'spiracy by th'A-M-A what ta keep us all sick," she emphatically declared.

"I think..." Gator slowly, calmly, laid out, "when your husband's b-... *testacles*, swell up ta the... size a... grape...fruits, ya really, really, *realllly* should think 'bout... goin' ta the doctor."

"You don't seem like you should oughtta be a-workin' hyear with a bad attitude like that!" the angry mother retorted. "I'll jes' take these a-hyear pills."

"Please, *pleeeease* think about it... or send him in, talk ta me."

"I don' *think* so."

Frankenstein's Paradox

    That night when Gator's Capri rolled down the dirt road he noticed a car across the road and there was light and a lot of loud noise coming from inside the once empty house. It was still loud, even inside his own house, hours later as he lay on the meditation pad, staring at the big yellow light globes of his ceiling fan. But it didn't matter. He couldn't sleep anyway, thinking about that guy's giant balls.

***

JD Hollingsworth

August 15, 1976

peep peep peep deedle deedle deedle peep peep peep
peep peep peep deedle deedle deedle peep peep peep

Gator awoke, looked up from the floor to one of the few remaining acoustic tiles overhead and thought, "Dammit..."

He was going in late to work so he could meet Anderson's handyman, Darnell, about fixing a leak in his bathroom again – which meant wrapping the pipe in more duct tape – but he was still hoping to sleep in a little later.

He rolled over and stood up then reached back down to the floor for his Camels and pants, which he slipped on and walked out onto the porch where he scratched his behind and lit the cigarette. He looked over to some motion beneath the water tower only to see Marie poking at something in the kudzu with her potato dibbler. Gator had time to kill, so slipped on his shoes and wandered over hoping Marie might tell him one of her fascinating tales to pass the time before Darnell arrived.

She would sometimes recall some simple remembrance, like of her father "...what a-had him four yoke a bottomlan' on th' Okgatalatchee an' were such a bodacious husban'man he could a-made thangs a-grow on a *rock*... Tha's a-whah mah patch a sallet be so great." On the other hand, sometimes she would threaten to take her grandpappy's Confederate pistol and shoot Gator dead for one reason or another, like when he had tried to take her picture or when she accused his car of trying to kill her Chinaberry tree. Then, sometime she would relate the unbelievable: he would never have guessed, for instance, that her little pug-mix dog that looked like Ernest Borgnine grafted to a bologna, had been miraculously birthed during – and apparently *by* – the tornadoes of '74. Marie remembered that as a cyclone passed through the nearby field, which, until then, had contained rows of more old abandoned mill houses,

"Land a Goshen, no one a-knows what a-happen back here... Oh 'at ternader wast jes' a-runnin' crost th' champaign an' th' house were a-shakin' an' a-rockin' lak mah Pappy's ol' tractor a-runnin' downhill an' 'en th' door jes' a-*blowed* off an' th' winders a-blowed out an' 'er'uz a bottl-a Squirt a-sittin' on th' sank an' 'at thang it jes' *a-burs' open* an' all 'at 'ere yeller pop a-sprays inta 'at ol' apple crate an' 'en, land's *sake*, if'n 'is hyear dog din't jes' a-*jump* out n'up on Pappy's peck-measure an' jes' start a-*dancin'* lak a communis'!"

Marie folded her arms out in front of her and began to spastically throw one leg, then the other forward, and laughed like a woodpecker. She caught her breath and continued,

"*Whooooo!* An'... an' Ah says 'Well... Ah'z a-gonna name *you* Percy,' an' 'e says, '*NO!* Mah name be *Pungo th' Secon'!*' wi'out a-droppin' a step...Ain't 'at raht?"

Pungo the Second became animated and sat up, smiling his Borgnine smile, snorted and sneezed and began excitedly walking in circles and wagging his tail: which for him meant wildly flexing his entire stubby bologna body from one side to the other.

"Pungo the Second?" Gator puzzled. "Why 'the Second'?... I mean... doesn't there have ta be a... a *'first'* for...?"

"Who m'ah ta tell a dog?" she shot back angrily.

But now, as he neared her beneath the tower she began to aimlessly blow upon a bugle. She trudged through the vines to another place below the rusted vessel and blew again then looked overhead and held her hand to one of the tower's supports as if feeling its temperature. When Gator reached the tower she stopped, spit a gob of snuff juice and looked at him. She removed her hand from the rusty steel and pointed to the tangle of kudzu and briars at her feet. A large rabbit sat there busily working a sprig of grass into its mouth.

"Ol' Mr. Coney got hisself a tanglered up in th' briars..." Marie related.

Gator laughed like a child and remarked, "Oh man that's fuckin' hilarious... like the story..."

Marie glared at him.

"So... ya granted him his freedom..." he said, feeling a bit uncomfortable.

"Freedom ain't a-granted... Jus a-taken or give back." She said with some irritation.

Gator cleared his throat, said, "I heard *that*..." then pursued the topic no further: besides he sensed this was all some sort of distraction.

"So... uh... So, ya seen the cat?" he asked.

Marie brightened and clucked, "*Ah hahaha!* I a-reckon he's a gettin' ready fer th' party!"

"*What?*"

"Yer malkin 'ere, he come over pert near ever day an' a-*riiiides* Pungo th' Secon' 'round lak a cowboy! We gots us a *ro*-deo! Heeeheeheeheehee!" She claimed. "They rides aroun' an' 'roun' th' garth!!! Whooeee! An' th' rest a us, we jes' a-*laaaughs!* "

"...*rest* of us?" Gator wondered.

She went on to claim that the cat "a-says he a-hates 'at 'ere stupid name what ya give 'im, an' Ah a-says, 'well 'course ya does! Yer name be *'Trav'ler!'* An' he a-says, *'Tha's right!!'*"

"*'Traveller?'* Ya mean... like... Robert E. Lee's *horse*?"

"I don' know. Ask *'im!*"

Darnell pulled up and Gator had to leave but keen for the tale to live on. As he walked away, he turned back and said, "I wanna hear more a this story..."

"Ain't no *story!!*" Marie yelled back angrily, and he now remembered that, to her, "story" meant an untrue tale.

Marie began to blow upon her bugle once more; Gator met Darnell at the door, let him in, then stood there on the stoop to light a cigarette.

Suddenly, "*Got* damn!" he felt a sharp burning pain in his back. He reached back grimacing and spinning around like a dog chasing its tail trying to see where it hurt. He gave up and went inside with the spot on his lower back feeling like a cigarette had been put out on it. Darnell had the duct tape out and Gator asked him to look at the burning spot.

"Look like ya got a *hole* in ya shirt."

"What about in me?"

"Uh huh, that too."

"Goddamn! What the fuck..."

He stepped outside and looked around. Had Marie shot him with that Confederate pistol because of what he said about her "story?"

No, he'd be dead. What the hell happened?

Darnell came out and said it was "finished." Gator went in and looked under the sink. By this time – the third "repair" – the duct tape on the supply line looked like a giant gall on a tree in the woods and water continued to weep from the seams.

"*Maannn...*"

For now he had to get to work, but he would figure out what was going on later: with *every*thing.

After work Gator stopped by Katy Lemonade's to study homeopathy.

"...so that's thirty X!" she explained.

"But... by that time..." Gator groaned with incredulity, "after that many dilutions, there wouldn't be any trace – at all – a what you say is the active ingredient. That's like a ratio a... a like, one ta ten ta the... *sixtieth* power... I don't even know what there's a *name* for that number..."

"I know. That's because water remembers."

"Remembers what?"

"What molecules've been dissolved in it."

"So this ain't science... it's magic."

"*Nooo...*"

"It remembers every molecule..." he went on with growing frustration at his lesson, "So, *ALL* water has had *everything* – ever – dissolved in it. So, it all remembers every mineral an' salt an' all the poisons... the chlorine – an' the pee – in the pool? An' the oil spills, the sugar in your coffee, grandma's Polident, an' the fish jizz, an' every *trilobite* turd an'..."

"Stop! Just what *you put in it*!"

"But if it... Aghhh... I can't do this anymore right now. Could ya look at somethin' for me?"

"Hmmmf. You're so negative."

"I disagree. But could you look at..."

"*Positive* about anything?

"Well, my glass is half empty... but it's lemonade!"

"Dude... *Serious* about anything..."

"Yes... But could you look at..."

""Yes... Okay... what?"

Gator turned around and lifted his shirt. "Is there a... a *wound?*"

"Oh, far out. Cool. There's like a little volcano."

"So a hole? In me?"

"Uh huh..."

"Is there anything in it?"

"*IN* it? ... Uhhhh Ohhhh I... I, *brrrrrr*... I can't..."

"Jus' poke at it."

"*POKE* at it?"

"Yeah, jus'... ya know?"

"Ohh*hhh*..." she whined and she poked, "*ewww... ewww... ewww... EWWW...*"

"Ouch!" Gator cried.

"Ohhh sorrrry... *ewww... ewww...* AHHH!!!" she screamed.

"What?"

"Ohhhhhh... something clicked!" she shuddered. "On my fingernail... *ewww grosss!* Things-*inside*-a-thiiings... ohhh *gross gross gross gross gross...*" and she shook her hands as if trying to fling water off of them.

"*Things inside-a things?*" Gator asked with a confused scowl.

"It's just this... this thing I've got..." she said, flustered, "'bout... things inside a things... don't ask..."

"Yeah, I won't. Whatever. Can ya... pick it out?"

"*Pick it OUT!?*"

"Yes, just pick it... with your nail..."

"Ohhhhhhhhh... Why are you doing this to... Oh... *ew... ew... ew... ew... ew...* AHHHH!!"

Something clinked on the floor and Katy jumped back from it.

"Ahh! Something fell out!" She jumped back more, holding her neck and pointing wildly at the floor. "*Right there! Right there! Right there!*"

"Jesus, Stop freakin' out."

"Ohhhh... *Things-insiiiide-a-thiiings*..." and she did a little dance and shook more water from her hands.

"Well," Gator pointed out, "it ain't *IN*-side any more."

"Oh... yeah... What is it?"

Gator picked it up and rolled it back and forth between his thumb and forefinger.

"It's a... *pellet gun* pellet... Varmint shot."

"Weirrrrrd. What's that mean?"

"It means somebody shot me."

"On purpose? Far out..."

When Gator got home there was more noise coming from the house across the road. He stood on his porch and saw there was a window partially open on the side of the house facing his, and he speculated, "Like... the book *depository*..."

He walked across the road and up on the noisy new neighbor's porch. He went to the door and knocked. The noise continued unabated. He knocked harder and the yelling stopped but the Lynyrd Skynyrd didn't.

"*WHUT?!?*" came loudly from inside.

"It's your neighbor... " Gator yelled over the music "across-the-road. *I-want-ta-talk-ta-you.*"

Sudden, wild laughter erupted from within, then, "Well... *howdy* neighbor!" followed by frantic giggling. Gator knocked again, more loudly. "Railroad Song" stopped playing and, in the silence that followed, Gator could hear male voices sputtering and trying to contain their child-like tittering.

"Jesus, fuckin'..." Gator began.

The door opened.

"'SUP, BUDDY PEG!!??"

It was Rifleman Duquesne.

"Git high, mother*fucker!!*"

And Rail Road.

It was Rail Road and Rifleman Duquesne: across the road... from him.

"What th' hell bro? Wondered when you'uz a-gonna git yer ass 'crost th' street!" Rifleman exclaimed.

"Did you *shoot* me?" Gator asked, dispensing with formalities.

Much hilarious laughter followed.

"Fuck yeah, motherfucker! How else we gonna git y'over hyear?" one of the interchangeable brothers demanded with genuine confusion.

"So you *shot* me?"

"Hell, mane, jus' ol' rat shot," the other snorted dismissively. "Got us a air rifle."

"Yeah, s'rong wit' ya, bro? *You* done los' yer edge, buddy peg. 'Sides we do this each other alla time. See?" said the first, and he turned around dropping his cut offs to present what looked like two Gouda cheeses embedded with caraway seeds.

"Sorry bro, we's jus' sayin' 'hello.'"

"Yeah, mane... Wait!" the dropped-trouser brother enthused, then hitched his pants back up and ran in the house, returning with a Crosman 760 Pumpmaster air rifle held out to Gator.

"Hyear, ya kin shoot us..."

"Yeah!"

"Go 'head!"

And they both turned around and dropped their shorts.

"No! Jesus... No..." Gator yelled, then froze for a moment, calmed and sighed, "I ain't gonna... *shoot* nobody. Christ," raising his hands up to the sides of his head

"Well, we'll a-do sumpin' fer ya."
"Yeah!"
"Yeah!"
"Yeah! We'll mow yer lawn!"
"Yeah!"

"No! I don't... Ya know what?" Gator said, calming down again. "Jus'... jus' don't shoot me... ... Okay?"

They had both turned back around, fastening their pants, "Awrite, mane."

"Alright..." Gator attempted to reassure, "Okay, look I'm really tired. It's... cool... weird, but cool, y'all are here an' all... An' I ain't even sure we're s'posed ta be... associatin'..."

"Whut?" they both said in unison.

"It's too much ta..." Gator went on, "Look, I jus' need ta go back an' get some sleep. Been a long, weird day. Okay. So... I'll see ya 'round."

"Okay, mane, take 'er sleazy..."

Gator walked away but stopped and, without looking back, said, "An' don't shoot me."

"Heard *an'* heard, buddy peg."

Gator got home and opened the box in his kitchen where he kept his reefer. It was gone.

"Fuck! *Per*-fect."

***

Frankenstein's Paradox

September 2, 1976

"Rent *TAHHHHM!*"

Here it was again, and with it, following the workings of his own internal gearing, Gator's personal astrolabe, sextant, corroded old Antikythera mechanism, John Anderson, arrived to once more proclaim the Music of the Spheres. Though this month he was a day late, so Gator questioned his own calendar.

The dollars Gator was now about to hand over seemed somehow devalued following the past few weeks of the Duquesne brothers shooting fireworks all night, cutting donuts with a dirt bike in the yard all day, yelling his name and whooping, "*Free Birrrd!!*" each time he drove by, and constantly going on about their endless, futile, attempts to defeat the ever-growing paper wasp nest on their front porch. Their home could now have been certified a toxic waste site from the Merck Index of chemicals that had been thrown, sprayed, hurled or otherwise applied to the hive: yet, the demon-faced hymenopterans built on.

And then there was the missing weed.

Anderson waddled up from a white Mercedes. He had two identical cars – aside from the color. When one broke down he drove around in the other while the first got fixed. This meant that the gold one was in the shop. That explained why Anderson had arrived a day late for his rent, and so restored Gator's faith in his celestial precision. It also meant Anderson was spending money on a repair right now, which would make what Gator was about to attempt difficult, if not impossible.

Originally Gator had felt the urge to "blow Anderson's hair back," regarding this issue, but upon reflection and meditation his cooler mind had prevailed and chosen the paths of misdirection and diplomacy.

huff snort "Rent *TAHHM!*"

One of the brothers was already up and circling the silver Honda XR75 around and around a radius with his left foot as its origin. A three-foot spray of mud and rocks followed the dirt bike around the moat they had excavated, which was already close to eighteen inches deep.

"Them fren's a..." huff " fren's a yose, pretty... pretty LOUD!"

"Yeah, they are."

"Says" smack snort "says they knowed ya" huff " knowed ya up in the... up in tha *SLAH*-muh." fart

"Yep."

"Needs mah" huff "mah MUH-ney now!" slurp "Spose ta done got it *YES*-tuh-dee!"

"Well, I'm very sorry about that, sir..."

Anderson seemed confused by the response and cautiously muttered, "Uh huh..."

"So... when Darnell was here last time," Gator began, "he took some... herbs... from my kitchen. So, I'm gonna keep twenty dollars a the rent... an' you can get it from Darnell."

Anderson stood motionless for a moment then uttered a fading "Uhhhhbs...?" snort

Then, as if in a trance, Anderson continued to just stand and stare straight ahead.

Hoping to force the deal through, Gator held out and fanned the forty-five dollars he had gotten all in ones and fives to make it seem like more, but Anderson continued to stare: trying to make sense of anything he had heard. A strand of drool began to rappel down from his lower lip. After another long moment he, without moving or blinking said,

"Uhbs? Whud a niggah be wan'in w' uhbs?"

"Don't know... maybe he cooks..."

Anderson became even more deeply locked in, catatonic, and Gator watched the strand of drool slowly elongate and begin to sway. After a minute or so, Anderson's hand, seeming to operate independently of his body, worked its way down to his zipper to, as usual – even in this trance state – extract his penis and begin to urinate in the grass as the drool rope lengthened.

At almost three feet long and swaying in a long lazy arc, the swinging strand of saliva reminded Gator of a Foucault pendulum. Anderson stood there with his penis out, giant eyeballs squinting through his thick, magnifying eyeglasses, and Gator thought, even if he had no idea where he was, that, with a decent watch set to Greenwich Mean Time and by measuring the angular speed of the drool's oscillatory precession in degrees per sidereal day – ω – thereby determining, via $\omega = 360 \sin(\phi)/day$, where ϕ is latitude – he could pinpoint the *exact* spot on Earth where this awful experience was occurring.

Anderson's tongue slipped around lubricating his lips. His hand, still as if a separate entity, now reached up to snatch the splayed bills then dropped to stuff them into a pocket.

Snort huff slurp "Dah-nell..." huff "Dah-nell fix tha'... tha' *PAP*...?" huff

Apparently unable to process the scenario, Anderson's brain had just skipped over it and moved on.

"Well..." Gator cautiously began.

huff "... whu'? Zit... still..." snort huff "... still a... a-*LAY*-kin'?" smack

"No. Yes...Well, not really... yet. But, I mean, I coulda done what he did. Hell, I coulda *fixed* it... Ya know... doin' that over an' over an' not *stoppin'* it's only makin' the floorboards rot worse." Gator complained. "Floor's saggin'. Whole things gonna cave in... Hell, ya drop a ping pong ball on the floor anywhere in the house, it'd roll t'wards the bathroom."

snort "*PANG pung bawl*?" huff "Wha'" smack "Wha' ya droppin' pang pung bawls on mah floah foah?" snort

"That's not... Never mind."

"Wha' wha'" huff "ya needs ta be a-doin" snort " that foah?" slurp

"...Yeah, it's fixed."

Huff "...well" huff "awrite then." snort "Don' knows 'bout ya a-droppin them pang pung bawls on the... on mah floah, tho'" snort slurp "B'lieve" huff "b'lieve ya needs ta" snort "ta *STOP* that."

"(...Jeez fuckin'...) Yeah, yeah...Don't worry. Never-happen-again."

huff slurp "Thank Ah needs..." slurp "Ah needs ta call" snort "ta call mah *LAW*-yah!" smack

His brain tired, Anderson yawned a big yawn and thumped his chest with his fist.

"Whoooo! Hyeah!" snort

He made a decent armillary sphere, but a baffling, disorienting human.

***

JD Hollingsworth

September 10, 1976

"*Shasta, it hasta be Shasta...*" Gator sang to himself as he hustled down Railroad Avenue, late for work.

"*Hey Gator!*" Joe Ray Garrison called from across the street, heading to Strickland's. "Jus' saw yer new movie! Hahahaha!"

"Haha! Yeah!" Gator yelled back with a dismissive wave. "Yeah right... Burt Reynolds, Gator... Okay, yeah..."

"What? No shaky puddin' no more?"

"Ha...Okay, Garrison..." Gator yelled back to Joe Ray, then mumbled, "Fuck off, asswipe," to himself and quickened his pace.

"*Shasta, it hasta be Shasta...*" Gator was singing again as he burst through the Health Hole door, where he stopped, noticing Katy Lemonade excitedly gesticulating with a fly-swatter and involved in conversation with a hippie's hippie, wearing pajama pants like Katy's, a tallit katan and sporting a scraggly mass of hair and one of those wiry but spotty beards – the kind with lots of bare patches that Gator attributed to dental x-rays. He also wore a bear claw necklace, feathers in his hair and – contrary to store rules – no shoes on his blackened feet.

Still, there was something about him Gator did not like.

Katy had, in fact, observed some time ago that Gator did not – with the singular exception of her – seem to care for hippies at all. After some reflection, he had said, "Well, hippies are... like dogs... ya know? Shaggy, eat weird stuff... track mud *all over* an', ya know, smell bad but mean well, I s'pose. So, lovable, in a dumb way... But, then they crap on the rug an' you gotta take a rolled up newspaper to 'em," and Katy just walked over to the bulk bins and ate a handful of carob raisins.

Nevertheless, now Katy enthusiastically introduced this new one to Gator as "the healer, Vernal Equinox." After this many months at the Hole, and of Marie's tales, he was over questioning anyone's or anything's name.

Katy informed Gator, "Vernal lives in a native... a *what*...?"

"*Wickiup*" the unkempt Equinox said, "by the flowing waters of the Okgatalatchee," and then clasped Gator's hand in, not so much a handshake as, a crushing dominance hold and, as he did, Gator instantly knew him to be a fraud, and more importantly, a beast. The way a dog can smell a soul of evil, the way a vampire knows one of its own, Gator's innate sense, honed by years of prison, knew that Equinox shared his own tendency to violence, but that it came from a deeper, darker place: not a shorting circuit or failing switch, but a fundamental part of his nature, his *being* – and that Vernal Equinox, in fact, relished it. As their eyes remained locked, Equinox also recognized the kinship, and he knew that Gator knew.

"People come from miles around to seek his wisdom," Katy proclaimed, "and his knowledge of the healing arts and herbalism!"

"Not just the plant kingdom, but animal as well," he corrected, without breaking his gaze at Gator.

"Zootherapy, using the gifts of our brothers who swim and fly and walk like us. Nature's bounty of restorative gifts may come from creatures as diverse as..." he intensified his glare "... *maggots*, or," then softening, he turned to Katy "or the misunderstood *Hirudo medicinalis*, the candiru, or the cleansing *Garra rufa*... This is why I have chosen the shores of the living river as the focus of my curative vortex."

Gator twisted his hand free.

"Oh sweet heavens, that is such a gift from the spirits." Katy gushed, near swooning.

Equinox then said that he must "hasten for the place of healing" to prepare for his evening's ablution and ceremony of thanks and, "Oh, you think I could start a *tab* with y'all? For my medicines?"

Katy said she didn't think Poshlost would allow anyone to start a tab that didn't have a brick-and-mortar business, or a bank account... or money, but that she would be happy – honored – to put it on her own tab and he could just pay her when he could.

"Your vibrations are pure and golden. Can I honor you 'til then with the gift of one my self-fashioned *xiāo* flutes?" and from the sack around his shoulder he pulled one of the lengths of PVC pipe he had stolen from a construction site and drilled with random holes. He placed it in her hands then pressed his palms together, gently bowed and backed out of the door turning his gaze towards Gator as he rolled away with a smirk of defiance.

Katy turned back to the room, looking through Gator. Her smitten vacancy and flute and fly-swatter gripping hands crossed over her breast was the image of a crook and flail wielding pharaonic mummy. She sighed and then examined the "flute" in wide-eyed wonder and began efforts to bring forth music from the purloined plastic cylinder, but, since it was, like its creator, a hollow sham, by the end of the day it had borne nothing but the sound of wasted wind through a hole.

On his way home from work Gator had his Capri blocked in the road by the Duquesne brothers in their uniform of cut off shorts and wife-beaters.

"Hey, mane, we're a-gonna go out an' get some pussy later." They always said that. "Wanna come?" That too.

"I don't know, Pie," Gator began, when the twin puckered his mouth and protruded his lower lip, sadly.

"I don't know... *Rail Road...*" Gator restated, and the young man beamed with pride.

"Kinda tired... man," he went on, "Maybe some other..."

"C'mon buddy peg...'" the brother protested, "We's a celebratin'. We done a-squirted 'at warsp nes' w'a *shit* ton a *Dub*ya-Dee Forty an' thank we a done done it this-a tahm!"

"Hot damn, yeah, mane!" Rifleman rejoiced.

Gator looked them both up and down and asked, "You guys get inta that poison oak over yonder again? I warned y'all 'bout playin' over there..."

One of the brothers looked down at the pink welts that speckled his and the other's arms and legs and proudly proclaimed, "Hell nooo, mane! We got th' *fuck* a-stinged outta us by alla 'em ol' pissed off warsps when 'ey all tooked off from th' Dubya-Dee!! Whoooweee! They-'Uz-*MAD!* But they's a-gone an' now we's a-goin' huntin'."

Gator hated being around guys who were bird-dogging: he found it embarrassing and gross. But they always failed and since, even from here in the road, he could see the big nest on the porch soffit – that had now grown to the size of a hubcap – was already swarming with wasps that were, even then, returning and take back their town, he felt sorry for the knuckleheads.

"Okay. But I'll meet ya there later. I need ta read some."

"*Whoooooo*weeee! *Hot* damn! Be jus' lak ol' times! 'Ceptin we kin drink an' ain't in prison!!... ... Wait... *read?*"

Gator parked and climbed up to his porch where he pushed away the ashtray on the wooden wire spool he used for a table and laid his burden down. He set aside the jar of Elmer's school paste and a haul of old magazines from atop the spool. Then, one-by-one, he raised and admired the hard, crisp and shiny and physics and engineering texts he had received in the mail at work so he might embark upon his plans to return to his studies and make something of himself.

He stepped inside and returned a moment later with another stack. He placed it alongside the texts and patted it like a dog. The Vitruvius, the Wingler, the Capra he had bought reminded him that this was all not just numbers, but music: music like any other, with meter and scale and movement and moment and harmony and rhythm and Pythagoras that graphed as beautifully as any score.

And he was taken back to the time he knew what he wanted.

Growing up, Gator's family was not the kind that could go on vacation, nor even a weekend trip: not like those folks on two-ditch roads could; certainly not to anywhere exotic like Cherokee or Myrtle Beach; not to even the relatively nearby Warm Springs or Brunswick.

Until the old man was hit with a mid-life crisis.

His old man – who *was* in truth an old man, having fathered both of his sons well into his forties – was a man of lofty and unfulfilled dreams and feared – loathed – the possibility of exiting this mortal coil having seen nothing beyond the flatwoods of the coastal plain and so dedicated the years following Roosevelt's birth to making some brief escape possible: to travel; to see things. Nearly a decade of backbreaking menial labor later, labor far beneath what his true capabilities might have brought him, and now nearly beaten down, James Jesse Franklin had saved just enough to make a single, near-cross-country, trip to visit his brother in Phoenix when young Roosevelt was nine.

His mother, Arlene, objected to travel, on spiritual grounds, as wasteful and to "seeing things' as covetous and against the lord's wishes and so stayed home. This freed J.J. and his sons Roosevelt and Woodstove to voyage unencumbered with guilt and breathe freely the fresh air of new lands.

From Utinahica to Albany to Dothan to Pensacola, where they picked up the Old Spanish Trail, it all looked like nothing the boy had seen before except for being the first - and only – time he saw the ocean. Then, there came in Alabama the great docks and bridges of Mobile Bay and the John H. Bankhead tunnel where Roosevelt could hardly believe they were traveling *beneath* the water. There were the great manufacturing facilities of the Ingalls Shipyards of Pascagoula, Mississippi and the Lake Pontchartrain Causeway in Louisiana, whose hum and endless rhythm of passing pilings and expansion joints were mesmerizing and, to him, even now, no less beautiful than the Roman's Pont du Gard.

Then there was a thousand miles of Texas and four hundred more of Arizona to Phoenix which, aside from vaguely reminding him of the landscape in that Road Runner cartoon he had seen before *Darby's Rangers* at the Bibbjoux Theater in Macon, held little of interest for him and he longed for more of the fantastic, futuristic worlds of Alabama, Mississippi and Louisiana, mere hours from his doorstep, that had only just fanned the spark of his imagination.

But then there were the dams.

Far from of Arlene's moral judgments, James Jesse, with giddy abandon, allowed himself the devilish extravagance, before heading the Nash Rambler back to Georgia, of a fugitive foray to Las Vegas where he got a room at the Riviera and neither drank nor gambled but did hand a bus boy a sawbuck to sneak the boys into the showroom to catch the Ritz Brothers: of whom all Roosevelt could think was, "what is these guy's problem?" But along the way, as an educational amelioration of his indulgence, J.J. did make a side excursion to the Parker Dam north of Quartzsite. The dam, with its humming substation, phalanx of high-voltage towers, and Speer-like colonnade atop the gently sweeping arch-gravity shell structure of the dam body holding back Lake Havasu was the single most impressive thing he had ever seen much less stood upon. But only a few hours later, as they approached Las Vegas and he stood upon Hoover Dam, nothing had ever moved nor would ever so move him as the dizzying view down the dam's face to the turbine's discharge from Lake Meade.

He saw the world differently from then on. The mighty and the mundane now held mysteries and mathematics within to be solved. Even the cornfields along their northern route home, rolling by like the spokes of a great and endless wheel hubbed upon the Illinois horizon presented puzzles of relativity and perception to analyze, and filled him with irrepressible wonder as they traveled.

To Woodstove's irritation Roosevelt subjected the old man to a catechism of conundrums such as, "If ya drove where we're goin', but in reverse... would we be goin' forwards?" and, "Does the road take you or do you take the road?" and, "Where is the first car on the highway!?" which, to give the boy a meaningful answer the old man understood he deserved, he pondered, then said, "It's where this road ends."

"Where is that?"

"...It's where the next one begins!"

"So... So it's all one big road?"

"I reckon it is Roosevelt. I sure do reckon it is."

This was the beginning of Roosevelt's brief affair with optimism.

Then he drowned.

The old man had come back home and died. And that was that.

But Roosevelt had come back from the dead and returned home; altered, but intact, and in spite of his detour he had persisted: he could conquer this thing. Katy's own reading of Gator's I Ching told of a great man's inner cheerfulness that allowed him to persevere. And now, the end of this old road he had traveled so long led to the beginning of another and he knew where it was going: to that thing of which he needed to be a part. It was just another puzzle, another equation to understand and to solve correctly.

All he needed was the answer. He didn't even have to show his work.

Now he sat before the instruments of his deliverance. He had, in the past, briefly considered returning to school, but life was then just a piece of old gum with the flavor chewed out and there was no point, no inspiration, for his efforts. But now he thought about Katy Lemonade. In spite of his feelings he had kept his mouth shut – but he thought maybe she knew – but still he hoped that maybe – maybe – if he could just become something... And, even though he had also always worried about his brain, his annoying constant companion, that embarrassing trouble-making friend each of us has but to which he was inexorably manacled, and of what it might do, and, so, worried about her, he had been doing so well lately at taming the viper at the top of his spinal cord, and hoped that if he kept it in its place and did return to school, and that success materialized, then keeping it under control might be even easier... with achievement... and someone, and a life, to look forward to.

And he thought maybe he'd be bringing her up out of... *this* – bringing her through to cooler things beyond – too.

He lit a cigarette and looked across the road to see the brothers hopping around and flailing at the furious social insects swarming them.

"Poor dumbfuckin' clodhoppers," Gator thought about how they did, in fact, always fail at romance.

Maybe it was the tattoos.

One of the inmates at Reidsville had a tattoo the twins very much admired and wanted for themselves. They brought The Original in to see Maori, the prison tattooist, who examined the artwork, then duplicated it perfectly on the brothers. The Original had L, T, F, and C tattooed, respectively, on the second through fifth proximal phalanges of the left hand and, similarly, E, S, U, and K on the right. According to The Original, one merely need sit across from "a lady," fold one's hands, and wait silently until the cleverness of the revealed sentiment – "LETSFUCK" – on the interlaced digits worked its magic. The Original claimed that it never failed.

And, perhaps, it might have worked for the brothers too but for one unobserved detail. Like the majority of the human population, The Original clasped his hands with the left hand superior. Sadly, the twins were part of the minority who clasp their hands with the right hand on top and therefore produced "ELSTUFKC" as their mating display. Whether Maori, The Original, or any other person realized this, they never said, and the brothers themselves remained clueless by their own observational talents. As this one piece of legerdemain was the sum total of their game, they, even now, remained loveless.

Or it could have been just because of who they were.

Either way, "poor dumbfuckin' clodhoppers."

But, as for Gator, he had these books. He could do it. He would take that big road, be a part of that dam after all. He had reason to celebrate.

The 441 White Line Fevers were loud that night.

Gator could not take his eyes off the steel player. He squinted and grimaced along with every chord change and note bend. "Those knee levers must be *hell*," he thought.

They were: particularly the second and third levers that operated by the knees moving *in*. Every time an E or the sixth string dropped, Gator would wince like a spectator at a particularly brutal boxing match. When the player dropped the full E to a B chord – pushing *both* levers in – and Gator saw him bite his lip and go cross-eyed, Gator empathetically went knock-kneed and did a little curtsey.

"Ohh...God... How does...?... Why doesn't he... ?" he thought, squirming, then heard,

"Now wxxt? Are yxx xxxxxxx?" from behind him through the music.

Gator looked back and saw Katy.

"What?" he yelled back over the noise.

"Now-What?" she yelled back *"Are-You-Dan-cing?"*

"Jus'-Watch-in'-This-Guy."

"Oh. Thx xxx yxx xxid xxx inxxxxx."

"What?"

"The-Guy-You-Said-Was-In-tense?"

"Yeah... In-tense-Pain!"
"*Him?*" Katy asked, confused.
"Yeah... Grape-Nuts."
"Grape-Nuts!?"
"Yeah.-Him."
"His-Name-Is-Grape-Nuts!?   ...   No-His-Name-Is-Mis-ter-Shep-herd."
"Never-Mind-I-Don't..."

"Thank ya folks," the band's singer announced over the PA as the music stopped. "We're gonna take a short break, an' we'll be right back with more a yer fav'rite tunes in jus' a little bit."

"Ohh.. great..." Gator said, sticking his pinky fingers in his ears and wiggling them.

Katy said, "Wow, they're loud tonight, right?"

"Yeah."

The steel player shuffled by and Katy complimented, "Hey, y'all are really great tonight!" He grimaced and moved on. "Wow, you're right, he's really limping... "

Gator groaned and Katy cocked her head back to the room and asked, "You see those two guys goin' at it over there before? Before the pigs hauled 'em off..."

"Yeah, *'look at those big men go*'" he sang, looking over his shoulder. "Dumbshits. Got their faces, then their asses, busted," and sang, "*In the jailhouse now...*"

"Wonder what it was about..." she wondered.

"About? Shit's never about nothin'... Real."

"Reckon *they* figured they had a reason."

"Yeah, everybody does," he surmised. People always *think* they got a reason... believe in what they're fightin' about. That's the problem with wars..."

Katy screwed up her face and thought.

"Know what's funny?" Gator interrupted her wonder. "I got rejected... draft... for tendency *ta* fight. Irony, huh?"

"You mean..."

"Brain shit..."

That... that what they call a... a 'section eight?'" she asked.

"You been watchin' *M*A*S*H*..."

"Okay... So, anyway... so don't you believe in anything?"

"Nothin' what I can't prove, an' not much worth fightin' about."

"Anymore..." Katy cooly, clarified.

"Su-ppo-sed-ly..." Gator enigmatically replied. "But now, jus'... goin' with the flow, ya know? I mean... life's a river, carryin' us along. Knows where it's been... it's like your water, it remembers, it knows. But, it's got a path... Knows where it's headed too, an' that's where you're goin'. Can't stop it. Fight it or float it, but that's where you're goin'. So... I'm jus'... floatin' like a leaf... Man."

"Yeah, man, that's cosmic..." Katy said, with a gentle nod of accordance and affinity. "Mellow," she went on, studying Gator's face, then, with sudden exuberance, burst out, "Hey, outtasight! Just noticed... if you had a mustache... you'd look just like Burt Reynolds. Right on!"

Gator scowled, very much like The Bandit.

"Hey man, what is up with all-a those heavy books you got today?" Katy said, her whims having changed.

"Huh? ...Oh. I'm gonna try... I'm goin' ta *go* back ta school."

"Is that important?" she asked, scowling.

"...Well, ta me... Improve myself... Never *had* nothin'... "

"You got yourself, and you're a good person."

"That's *all* I got," He specified. "I wanna make somethin' a myself, build somethin'... from *me*. Not be at the mercy a people. Like Poshlost. But... I wanna have a house, land... jus' a piece a dirt... somethin' what they can't take away."

"Physical things are the only things they *can* take away, ya know?" she said, smiling kindly.

"You sound like Poshlost now..." he unkindly distracted.

"Ouch! But they can't get what's inside you... what *is* you," she went on nonplussed.

"They can take your dignity... I know that."

"Didn't you lose that... yourself...?" she posed with, for her, a startling directness. "I mean, what you did. When you *did* fight. Lost your control... Prison..."

"That was strangled outta me first," he lamented, looking down at his beer. "First got the wind knocked out... then, no wind... ta hold back the water, then... *Anyways*," he sighed, "I keep myself locked up now... YOU though... you let people too far in. Too much access."

"I like to have an open heart."

"Ya don't protect yourself. Ya should leas' keep the chain on the door"

"If you keep the chain on the door when you open your heart they only get their hands inside."

"So... jus' leave the door open?" he griped. "Let 'em the whole way in? *You* have yourself too, an' *you're* a good person an' still, I think ya go lookin' for... somethin' ta make ya feel better 'bout yourself – for *some reason* – an' then..."

Frankenstein's Paradox

She looked sad.

"I'm sorry..." Gator felt awful, he had hurt her, and that hurt him with an empathy he had never known before. "I didn't mean... Okay, well, sure, yeah... there's nothin' wrong with... but... leas' keep the chain..."

"You're right... 'Katy bar the door,'" and she still managed another kind smile, because that was who she was.

Unable to communicate his regrets, Gator went on, far more openly than he had in years about himself, "Sorry... People jus'... *I can't jus' keep doin' the same things, makin' the same mistakes... over an' over. Hell, everybody* does. Hurtin' themselves... hurtin' people 'round 'em. But, I don't know... Maybe... *seein'* that... somethin' good'll come a it."

"Is that like Frankenstein's thing? Like... no pain, no gain?"

"No... That 'no pain, no gain' thing's jus' a choice... work hard, succeed, blah, blah. That – that... paradox or whatever – is... goin' through somethin'... somethin' ya fear, ta end up with somethin' ya want enough ta *face 'The Fear.'* Implies conquerin'... a triumph... Ya know... Ya overcome... without the fear there can be no overcomin'... ...But... ya know... it' aint like this is a thing with a set a rules... like the sausage rules... or anything."

"*Sausage* rules?? What are you..."

"Nothin'. I'm jus' sayin' it ain't somethin' I... worked out or... or put a lotta thought inta... Jus'... somethin' dumb I said."

"But, I dig it."

"Okay, well, then, I guess... I guess now I'm talkin' 'bout doin' the same *wrong*, destructive, things over 'n' over... Things with results ya *don't* want... an' stoppin' it. But, then the 'good'... is fixin' the problem. But, ya know, that's even harder than facin' *'The Fear.'* Maybe, sometimes, it's... *im*-possible. Even if ya try an' try ta... get rid a it... like, ya know when you're sweepin' an' some little piece a crud jus' keeps bouncin' back at ya?"

"Yeahhh," Katy laughed, " But I don't think that's..."

"Yeah, okay, I know... But... but if the problem is... *yourself*. So what do ya do? *Okay! Okay...* Yeah, okay... stickin' with the Universal mythology, it's like Larry Talbot. Larry Talbot cannot *not* be the Wolf Man..."

"This is *universal* mythology?"

"Yes, it is... but Talbot cannot *not* be the Wolf Man, an' when he is, he kills his friends an' shit. His repeated bad behavior hurts people an' he can't stop... maybe... maybe *none a us* really can. So what do ya do? This is... this'd be... *Talbot's Dilemma*! Stopping

Talbot's lycanthropy's hard as facin' Frankenstein's fear. Harder! But he's a good man. Tortured but... *good*, an' he's gotta fix the problem... by any means necessary. So he saves his friends... Since he can't *not* be the Wolf Man... He sacrifices. He chains hisself ta the radiator. That's not always the answer. But at least... At least, if ya *know* you're a beast... ya chain yourself ta the radiator..."

"You-are-a-doofus."

"But gallant."

The White Line Fevers were back and playing the organ opening from Billy Swan's "I Can Help."

Katy said, "X lxxv thx xxxx!"

"WHAT?"

"*I-Love-This-Song! This-Is-The-Best-Song-Ever!!*" she yelled.

"Me-Too. Makes-Me-Want-Ta-Go-Ro-ller-Ska-tin'."

"Ha-Ha. We-Should-Dance!"

"Oh...No-I-Don't-Do-That."

"C'mon!"

Katy placed her beer on the bar and picked up Gator's hands to pull him from his stool as she slithered backwards, but he would not budge. Still gripping his hands so tightly he could feel both of their heartbeats, she continued her serpentine dance, then leaned in, straight-backed, and pressed his own sweating hands to his temples. She closed her eyes and, ever so slowly tilting her head, moved towards his expectant, but panicked, face. Just as he feared their lips were about to meet, she veered to the side, lifted a hand away from his ear, placing her lips to it and breathed the words, *"C'monn mannn... Dannccce like nobody's... waaa-tchinnn'!"* that spread like steam across his cheek and down his neck, where his hair stood on end. She lingered, breathing, only long enough for Gator to understand the warm, moist, urgency that dwelled there. She leaned back, loosened her grip around his hands to interlace her fingers with his, and again began to sinuously swivel her hips and roll her shoulders, smiling coyly, leering at him beneath lids too heavy with desire to fully lift.

"*I'll-Jus'-Go-Where-No-Body-Is-An'-Not-Dance...*" Gator – again, loudly – demurred.

"*Don't-Be-Such-A-Bow-Tie-Daddy,*" she yelled in return, then, still loudly but somehow with the air of whispered intimacy, *"You-All-Locked-Up? Not-Just-The-Chain?"*

"*I-Guess...*"

"*Afraid-I'll-Get-My-Hannnds-Insiiiide?*" she said with a different, sly, smile, dropping her chin to her breast, and popping her eyebrows twice, then sang, *"It-Would-Sure-Do-Me-Good-To-Do-You-Good... Lemme-Help...*" along with the band.

Gator could only respond with the tortured grimace of adolescent insecurity. She de-linked their fingers, dropping his hands to his embarrassingly respondent lap and backed up a few feet, all the while continuing her subtle but sensuous dance. Waving from side-to-side like the Sapera's cobra, she looked him dead in the eyes, licked her lips and mouthed the words, "*Come onnnnnnn...*"

He mouthed back "Don't dance..."

Katy shrugged and turned to dance away, but looking over her shoulder and gyrating her narrow hips for his benefit until swallowed by the crowd and he could, at last, no longer see her.

Gator killed his beer, adjusted his crotch, then got up and left the bar. In the parking lot he ran into Dwayne Sparks from his old roofing crew who asked where he was going.

"Goin' *hooome*."

"Yeah? A'hm goin' ta Miss Her."

"You an' me both, buddy..."

"Thought y'uz leavin'..."

Back at the house, Gator sat and smoked on his porch, serenaded by the bush cricket call and response metronome sawing away up in the Chinaberry tree and from the water oaks over by the twin's shack, where a single, rare, night-calling cicada also rasped a long, mournful plea for summer's last dance. As he pulled on his Camel and unknowingly bobbed his head to the insect's rhythm, he told himself he had done the right thing. He wanted it to be right. He respected her, was looking out for her: for both of them. He didn't want to be another night she regretted the next morning.

There was the sound of a car and noise across the road as the twins got back from somewhere. Then there was the puttering sound of another car and the sound of female laughter. The Duquesnes had finally found some dyslexic barflies somewhere he thought with genuine appreciation. There was riotous laughter and he heard, "Oh my God. That is the *funniest* thing I have *ever* heard in my *entire* life!" and his heart sank as low as it had ever sunk: to an even deeper and darker place than when he first passed through the rehabilitating gates of Reidsville. He told himself he must be mistaken: that Katy didn't; she couldn't. But the bugs in the trees told him he was wrong.

***

IV

JD Hollingsworth

January 19, 1977

In January there came a freakish wave of "yankee winter" through middle Georgia. It had actually snowed – not like in '73, but there was snow on the ground in Utinahica. The temperature dropped into the low single digits one night and Gator had moved off the floor to the neglected bed, since, with the house being up on brick piers and open beneath, the uninsulated plank floor was, quite literally, freezing. When he awoke in the morning and went, wrapped in a cocoon of blankets, to use the bathroom he found the toilet a frozen rink and nothing flowed from the faucet. He got a propane torch and crawled beneath the house to thaw the copper and galvanized pipes, being careful to keep the torch in motion along the length of the pipe so as not to create a trapped pocket of thawed water to overheat, go gaseous, and explode in his face.

Now he had water to drink at least and, for the time being, would just follow Anderson's lead and urinate in the yard. He wasn't sure about the other issue, but would deal with that when it came. He went out onto the porch to smoke and take in the rare sight of snow on the field beyond Marie's place, on the skyrocket tower, and over on the tops of the old empty mill buildings with their black, bottomlessly vacant windows. They made him think of Dickens and Olde London Towne and, in its rarity, he beheld now how sound-dampened landscapes under snow and iron gray skies cast no shadows in the color-desaturated light that came from everywhere and nowhere. Wisps of loose snow whipped and slithered in sinuous bands over the ground like lost spirits in the wind that came and went. He thought it all ghostly, otherworldly, melancholy – lovely – then shuddered with an unease that seemed borne from more than mere cold.

Then, not twenty feet away, standing among the twisted vines and dead stalks that rattled in the wind in Marie's yard, he saw The Ghost of Christmas Yet-to-Come. He jumped and dropped his cigarette.

The wasted figure in a dark, flowing cloak, and whose draping cowl obscured its face, stood clutching itself. Gator could only open his mouth; move his jaw. Then, it ominously raised an arm from a hunched shoulder and lifted a bony, quivering – condemning – finger to him.

It spoke: "You got warter?"

Poor Marie, wrapped in an old army blanket, stood shivering and thirsty in the snow.

"Oh, fuck... Yeah, yeah I do! Yeah, hang on."

"Thank ya, Gater... Mah pump spigot gone frore ta solid... Sprang's hard two hands deep. Ah come nigh a-dried up dead from the thirstses," came weakly from the hood.

"Sorry... I..."

"Ah kin fetch ya a cruse what ta fill..." the shivering spirit offered.

"No, I'll fill up a couple-a milk jugs. Bring 'em out in a minute."

"Oh, thank ya," Marie croaked and Pungo the Second burst through her door to shoot into the yard and begin his usual frantic, energetic circling, stopping occasionally to shake his head and sneeze, then run around some more. At least he was smart enough to eat snow.

When Gator came back out with the two plastic jugs, Marie had returned inside. He, for the first time, now tremulously ventured onto her porch and called through the screen at the still open front door. Through the screen he saw Pungo the Second run into the front room, stop, sneeze, and run back into the dark rear of the house, his long nails clicking on the hardwood.

"Come own in, Gater, an' thank ya," echoed from somewhere in the back.

Come in? In Marie's house? Noooo.

"I'll just leave these at the door here," he begged off. "Okay, so.... I'll see ya. Keep warm."

"No! Brang 'em ta th' spence!" She insisted. "They's heavy..."

Jesus. "O... Okay."

He pulled open the creaking screen door and stepped inside. The air was sour. It was dark, but beyond the small parlor where he stood he could see a faint amber light leaking through a partially open doorway. He crept slowly towards it and pushed in its heavy raised-panel door as he crossed the threshold. In the light of an old kerosene hurricane lamp he could see Marie, still in her army blanket but unhooded, and her usually braided hair was down and flowing over her shoulders and much longer than he had thought. Pungo the Second sat next to her, panting. The room seemed much, much larger than it should be, and the ceiling far higher than he ever could have imagined. The room was too large and tall to even fit *in* the house. It was disconcerting.

As his eyes adjusted to the fuel oil light he could see the walls were covered in old clocks each stopped at a different hour and the room was filled with pieces of Second Empire furniture, very fine furniture, around whose every leg and foot was a puddle of frozen urine: around the legs of that *confident* chair; around those of that ornately carved spinet; that fainting couch; and, behind him, about the feet of that wing ba- *HOLY Fucking Shit!*

There was another person in the room.

Gator dropped one of the jugs.

"Tha's awrite," Marie said. "Ya kin jes' put 'em raht 'ere."

Sitting in the wing back chair he had looked past when he entered the room was... a child, a girl.

Wearing a red and white striped sweater, poodle skirt, and plaited hair, which seemed somehow... anachronistic, there sat a young, very pale, girl who stared intently at Gator.

Frozen with shock Gator could only stare back.

She only smiled a – menacing, he thought – tight smile and looked at him with burning, glassy eyes.

As the adrenaline shock had caused his own eyes to instantly and fully adjust to the dim, he looked more intensely.

Were they... *glass* eyes?

No, it... she... it... was... real. She was *looking at* him. He could see it; feel it.

Then, "No..." he attempted to reassure himself, "it's a big, creepy, *incredibly* life-like... doll? But..."

Marie walked over to where he stood and he bent to put the other jug on the floor without breaking eye contact with... whatever it was. He was *sure* the eyes followed him as he bent and stood again. He could not take his eyes off of... "her."

"Ohhh, thank yooo s'much, Gater. I don' mine none ya a-comes from th' bridewell..."

"Uh huh..." he said, without turning away from the girl.

"Trav'ler done tole me."

"Okay..."

"But y'ain't no blackguard."

"No."

"Lemme gives ya sump'n' fer a-hepin' me out."

'Uh huh... No... *No! God, no.*" he said snapping his attention back to Marie. "Wait, no... really," and he held up his hands waving away her offer, knowing that she was about to retrieve the change purse she kept hanging on a string down somewhere between her pendulous breasts or beyond, and which she always reeled up from the best-left-unthought-of regions to pay him for the cans of Tube Rose snuff or bottles of Squirt soda he picked up for her at the Food Bag. "Please, please. You don't..."

But she was already reeling it in.

She reeled and reeled and he wondered, "Where the hell is that thing comin' from?" while still shooting suspicious glances at the child/doll – who stared back fervidly – almost... *hungrily* – *at* him.

Finally, the little plaid poke appeared above Marie's collar and she unsnapped its clasp to extract a folded dollar that she stuffed into his pants pocket – keeping her hand there a little too long, and giggling, "Ah a-gots mah han' in a han'some squire's pocket, heeheeheehee."

The "girl" watching made Gator embarrassed and his unmanageable hindbrain went into full flight mode.

"Gotta go, get home..." he blurted, pulled Marie's hand from his pocket and headed for the door looking over his shoulder: irrationally fearing that a doll may be pursuing him. "Gotta go!" he stammered. "... f-feed the the c-cat."

"Trav'ler's *here!*" Marie called out.

"Okay... tell 'im I said, 'hello.'"

He had almost made the porch and was reaching for the door, when Marie – somehow now directly behind him – suddenly grabbed Gator's arm to stop him dead in his tracks and hold him fixed with remarkable grip strength. He turned to look at her, then over her head to the grinning simulacrum, still staring from the shadows of the dim yellow light.

"Firs' dozen night a-rule th' twelvemonth," she said, staring intensely into his eyes.

"Yeah...?"

"Thas' wha' mah Pappy a-said."

"Uh huh..."

"One day fer e'vr month."

"Uh huh..."

"Firstest day th' year wast *cold*."

"Yeah?"

"So this-a month cold."

"No kiddin'?" His gaze fixed upon the child to see if it moved or blinked or – God forbid – rose from the chair. His neck hair stood on end.

"Nest month be nermul."

"Yeah...?"

"March... be a wet un... but not fer long."

"Uh huh..." Maybe it was an actual, human head on a...

"But sprang... sprang a-gonna be dry... Like a ol' bone."

"Sure... Yeah..."

"Seventh day were stormy... July, watch out... Be a big wind... maybe a ternader. Refill th' sprang..."

"Okay, well, see ya, Marie..." He pulled away through the slamming screen door and hurried across her porch.

"Keep yer door closed!" Marie called out has he ran, slipping in the snow, back to his steps.

"Way ahead a ya!" he called back, as he pushed through that door.

Gator kicked away the cut-up magazines, photographs and scraps of colorful paper of his collaging, ignited the deadly space heater in a sudden flash of accumulated gas, then plopped in a chair.

"Should never a watched that *Trilogy a Terror* thing..." he thought.

He sat there smoking and thinking of the tea parties and rodeos Marie said went on over there and he imagined his cat riding Pungo the Second around and around the yard while Marie laughed and the grinning, hungry-eyed doll-child clapped its hands and stomped one foot like a square dance caller and he shuddered.

The cat came into the room by one of its secret entrances, crept like a nun along the wall, then padded to the center of the room where it sat to stare at Gator.

Gator stared at the cat.

They stared at each other.

"*So...* Mr. Whiskerton J. Stinkbottom the Third...."

The cat stared.

"So... *Traveller* ..."

The cat blinked a long, slow blink of affirmation, then stood up and walked away behind Gator.

Gator turned his head over his shoulder and yelled, "What the *hell* goes on over there!?"

***

Frankenstein's Paradox

As bitter cold as it was, as hard as the pipes were, the coldest, hardest and most bitter thing in the corners of his winter – or that year, or since prison – was that Katy Lemonade was married. She had impulsively chosen to plight her troth to the brutal sham healer, Vernal Equinox, and now parked her old Volkswagen, adorned with its Herbal Essences shampoo Beetleboard, by his teepee on the river. This, and that Equinox used the Health Hole as his source for ingredients – for which he never paid – to render his nostrums, caused him to be a regular and much-despised part of Gator's life. Aware of Gator's hatred and of their shared tendencies, Vernal would force interaction with a smarmy outward presentation of sodality and brotherhood.

Like that time he sauntered up, in Katy's warm coat and wearing a sarong and, with his disingenuous, if handsome, smile, clasped Gator's hand with both of his in a soul-brother handshake saying, "Peace brother, how goes your life-journey today?"

"Yeah, it's a real hip trip, Daddy-*O*. I'll send ya a postcard," Gator smarmed back.

"Ha HA! Far out, far out." Equinox chuckled. "Say... you seem really uptight. Your aura is, like," he raised his forearm as if to shield his eyes, "raging red and... and *darrrrk* blue... frustration... because of... of your desire to take *control*... but you just... *can't*."

"Hmmm, well, yours is *darrrrk* brown."

"Ha HA, yeah... No, there is no dark brown."

"Oh there's a great deal of brown. Right up ta your eyes," and Gator held his hand at his own, somewhat higher, eye-level.

"Okay, well, far out?" Equinox went on, seemingly unaffected. "Who am I to question your visions? But you should brew some chamomile and passionflower tea. Help you relax and sleep. Don't steep it more than three minutes though, man, you'll disrupt the sāttvik and the tea's natural harmonic vibrations of 558.92 megahertz..."

"Brother, ya *suuure* can shovel it high, can't ya?" Gator to came back to Vernal, who he saw was wearing a grubby T-shirt beneath Katy's coat that read, "A Man of Quality is Not Intimidated of a Woman of *E*-quality."

"Just saying people... *you* in particular... need to watch your vibrations," Vernal carried on in a soothing but arrogant tone.

"Well, sure wouldn't want *that*..."

"No, man, you wouldn't... you need all the beneficial vibes you can get."

"Well, I sleep fine." Which was true, as long as he was on the floor.

"Alright, that's mellow man... mellow. But in that case," he reached into the sporran hanging around his waist and retrieved one of the small muslin cinch sacks he had salvaged from cases of shoplifted Gold-Nuggets bubblegum, to fill with herbs, "this sachet is filled with mugwort, if you place it beneath your pillow it will give you vivid dreams!"

"So will malaria..."

"Ha HA! I'll dig ya later... *brother*."

Equinox walked away and, for the first time since they began speaking, broke eye contact.

Gator muttered, "...place *you* 'neath a fuckin' pillow'..."

Equinox stopped at the register and asked Katy Lemonade to put his items on her ever-growing store tab, planted a big long kiss on her lips and, as he rolled backwards out the door, shot Gator a peace sign and, again, flashed his hateful, disingenuous smile.

"Wow, you guys were really rappin' it up, man! I'm SO happy my two favorite guys are such buds!"

Far from buds, they were mortal enemies. Gator knew, from men like Vernal he had known before, and from the recently dwindling supply of hippies that had once busied the store, that those who portrayed themselves as the most enlightened were those to be trusted the least, and in particular, those who made a show of being the most behind women, were the ones most likely to be lurking there with a club, and so he knew that Vernal's ERA shirt was mere deceptive coloration; the flashing lure of an anglerfish; the sweet but deadly nectar of an insectivorous plant – only there to beguile his prey.

What was worse, in addition to merely recognizing Equinox to be a vain and violent man inside, Gator knew – saw, as well as any one with a pair of eyelids that raised could see – that Katy was suffering for it. Not only had her natural life affirming and joyous effervescence withered, even replaced outright by melancholy and sometimes a sadness that crushed Gator, but there were the bruises. There were often red marks or scratches on her face and arms, bruises around her wrists and once even the black eye she mindlessly attributed to walking into a door at home: a home that was a teepee.

And, unless he knew, for sure – he *saw* – there was nothing he could do. He couldn't even bring himself to ask. Still, to not crush Vernal Equinox into a soothing extract and sleep with a tea brewed from his bones was the hardest test he had yet had to pass.

***

v

JD Hollingsworth

Early May, 1977

Spring was dry. Like a bone.

By the wondrous rhythms of Nature, the angry orange wasps returned that spring and began a new nest by the door near the one that had plagued the Duquesnes the previous summer. By the end of June, and as Independence Day neared, it had already been soaked with gasoline, moonshine, Ronsonol, Gunk, Gumout Carb and Choke Cleaner, Pine-Sol, paint thinner, Thunderbird and Southern Comfort, and all of which the sting-spangled brothers had enjoyed drinking or huffing during their extermination campaign. Still, the colony of hexagonal paper cells had grown to the size of a healthy apple pie, and every day Gator was entertained by the manic marionette show of Rail Road and Rifleman dancing to the insect's tune.

Nevertheless, "poor dumbfuckin' clodhoppers."

***

peep peep peep deedle deedle deedle peep peep peep
peep peep peep deedle deedle deedle peep peep peep

Gator walked down the stairs to his yard repeating, "peep peep *peeeeep*... peep peep *peeeeeeeeeep*..." mockingly.

Though still irrationally uncomfortable being too close to Marie's house, when he saw her there at the far corner of the garden, standing still like a statue, her back to Gator and the world beyond, he wanted to investigate.

She was looking down to the dried-up spring. For once Pungo the Second just sat quietly at her side looking the same way. She was surrounded by butterflies and a pair of painted ladies and a spicebush swallowtail sat upon the crown of her head mechanically opening and closing their wings to the sun and probing her gray braids with uncoiled proboscises in search of moisture to sip. Gator approached from the side, and Marie, usually aware of everything around her, seemed oblivious of his approach.

But she knew.

"Groun's a-desiccated, like ol' Jack Tar's salt pork," she said without turning her head.

"*Desiccated??* Dang... But, yeah. Been dry... like ya said."

Marie, as was her wont, once more burst into song,
>"An' I pray with th' comin' a each dawn
>>that this a-crop killin' drought'll be gone
>>>You can dam up th' water
>>>>an' shut th' wind out
>>>>>But a man ain't a-been born'd
>>>>>>what can dee-stroy a drought"

"Guthrie?"

"Dudley..."

"So..." Gator went on, "I always wondered... is this *the* spring? The *'Mill Spring'* spring?"

"The sprang ist th' sprang, an' th' ditch ist th' valley..."

"Oh-kay... So... they ran... machinery... off... *this?*" he puzzled suspiciously.

"*Machines?*"

"*Yeahhhhh*..." Gator mumbled to himself. "So... Ain't much drop or... motive power..." then turned back to Marie, "There a... bigger stream out there?"

Marie moved her hand away from her slowly, as if pushing back a ghost, "It a-goes down... what's it's a-nature..."

"Seeks its level..." Gator re-phrased.

"*Out there*... Things a-goes down... a-moves on...On ta th' crick on ta th' river on ta th' sea on ta th' middl'a th'earth... Things a-moves on ta th' center a all things. Always a bigger crick..."

"We still talkin' 'bout the spring?"

"Sprang's a-dried up. Ain't a-goin' nowheres 't'all."

Gator shielded his eyes and looked up behind him to the water tower and contemplated, "Wonder if *that* thing's full a water..."

Marie looked overhead to the sky and reassured, "Up there always a-full a water. Come a time... time's a-comin... when it a-fall agin ta th'earth. Fall ta the earth fer th' tilth... Bring change. Now all's a-drought parch'ed an' thirstin' lan'... But soon," she looked at Gator, "Soon... it'll a-fall..." She paused, then asked, "Gater... ?"

"Yeah..."

"How's ya a-come ended up in th' gaolhouse?"

"Ehhhh... Tail... got caught in a crack..."

"*Heeheehee*. Ah trows 'at 'ere crack a-done come back 'n' a-bit ya a heap," she chuckled.

"I got a long tail."

"*HAhahahaha!* Now, Pungo th' Secon'... he'uz a-born'd wi' a bob-tail."

"Sadly, I was not. I kinda got it worked out now. Things'll... be alright now."

"Boast not a t'morrow..." she cautioned.

"Yeah, don't wanna jinx it," he agreed. "But it was a helluva climb, though... Still hangin' on."

"He what a-knows th'almighty an' do good hast th' most trustworthy handhold."

"Yeah..." Gator held his hand up and clenched it, as if holding tight, then looked at it: at the fist. He was making Jericho's black power salute and smiled broadly. "Yeah... Yeah, man! Tight!"

***

Frankenstein's Paradox

Early June, 1977

    Around mid-day Gator caught a glimpse of something speeding past the Health Hole window followed seconds later by a group of children dashing by and a ruckus down the street. He stepped outside and looked to see a chubby child – presumably the speeding object – down on the sidewalk and a few other children tossing a pair of glasses back and forth in a game of keep away while chanting, "Fatty, fatty, name is *'Patty!'*" Gator's blood began to boil and he charged the startled children who scattered like leaves from a sudden gust. A single, more courageous child, stood his ground to yell, "Patrick's a fat ol' pig-in-th'-mi- *aaahhhhh!!*" just long enough to realize the mistake he had made, drop the glasses and bolt just before Gator could drop him.

    Gator slowed and turned to walk lazily back. He stooped, picked up the glasses, wiped them off and handed them to the boy pulling himself up from the concrete.

    "Y'okay, sport?" he asked.

    The child rubbed his nose, put his thick, heavy glasses on, looked up at Gator with giant blue eyes and said, "You go ta... You go ta *HALE!!*" and himself turned to run away yelling, "*Jailbirrrrd!*" as he fled.

    "Well... *that* was uncalled for," Gator said, then turned back to the Health Hole.

    At the door he met the UPS man dropping off a large and heavy box. Gator signed for it, lugged it in and was immediately pushed aside by Todd Poshlost who excitedly began to pull at the flaps of the box. Inside that box was another box with a line drawing of the espresso machine it contained.

JD Hollingsworth

"Really?" Gator asked bemusedly.

"Yes... Really." Poshlost concurred. "This promises to be a paramount boon to our in-store hospitality sector, a major, major potential for increased sales... The longer patrons remain, in the store, at the café, the more they spend on ancillary product, and the variety we can now offer, well... well... well... " Poshlost fell uncharacteristically speechless.

The sad fact was that business at the Health Hole had been dropping off steeply over the past months and few even came in to just buy coffee *beans* anymore, much less sit at the "café" – a single table with the view of the F.T. Arbuthnot welding shop – and sip it, and those who in the past had had never spent an additional dime.

Poshlost dragged a metal shelving unit – half of the pair he had purchased for the office after abandoning the installation project – out of the back and directed that Gator, in his capacity as "facilities and building systems manager," get about to setting-up and learning to operate the gleaming contraption.

Gator walked off grumbling, "...big ass cords, handles, knobs, pipe-fittin's, pressure dials... I don't know, man. Looks like... like some kinda... *sub*-marine controls or somethin'..." to himself, even as he set at tackling the job.

Soon enough, though, Gator announced that as far as he could tell the machine was operational and Katy, Poshlost and the Adventist woman with her mute, sniffling children came over to observe its maiden run.

"Anyone else wanna try this?" Gator asked, " ...'cause I don't know what I trust it much."

"Truuuulllly?" Poshlost groaned.

"Well, hell... Ya got water... electricity, all goin' inta this... this pressurized... *vessel*..." he said, stepping back and waving his hands around the glorified coffee pot. "What if somethin' got... I don't know... all *crossed*-up?"

He thought he was being entertaining, though, as was often the case, he was merely confounding people.

"Well," Poshlost said, "that would be, as they say, 'on you,' now wouldn't it?"

"Okay..." Gator went on, "Well... cross your fingers – hope ya don't see a flash a light with a articulated skeleton, an' hear a xylophone play as my bones rain ta the floor!" and he turned around to smile expectantly at the audience of five.

Which all stood silent and wooden-faced until, after growing red, Katy's scrunched up and finally snorted a blast of snot which made her laugh harder. She and Gator beamed briefly. Their eyes locked for a moment and they both fell silent, grew straight-faced and chastened.

Gator cleared his throat, turned on the machine and went through the rigorously detailed, almost ritualized process of squeezing out a tiny cup of muddy water and topping it with foam. He ground and flushed and tamped and heated... and it was all somehow familiar and soothing to him... it was science. No, it was lab work, which, in a way, he loved more: the precise use of knowledge, materials, units, equipment, instruments...

- 18 g of coffee
- 9 bars of pressure
- 25 second pour
- 93° Centigrade water – no more than 50 ppm dissolved calcium, magnesium...

A few drops of amber fluid began to half-heartedly trickle from the cup spouts, and grew to two lazy streams that ran for a moment then fizzled to a dribbly stop. Gator felt a sudden need to pee but instead raised the tiny cup, holding it up to the light like a scientist in a television commercial, then placed it on the metal counter. He poured some milk into a glass jar he had found in the back and stuck it under the steam nozzle where it hissed and gurgled and finally wailed like a mournful wind around a haunted house, then decanted the slurry into the tiny cup, finishing with a little flourish that left a dainty white spiral on top of the caramel brew.

"Seems ta all be in... crackerjack order," he said, then, without turning around returned to the back room.

There was no applause, though Poshlost did loudly sigh, "I find you ever so difficult to deal with..." as Gator walked away.

Gator didn't bother to respond and in the back began to gather up the packaging material, flattening the boxes, putting the owner's manual and the warranty card on Poshlost's cluttered desk.

Katy appeared in the doorway, cup in hand, "This is righteous, man."

Gator looked up, then back to his chores, "Thanks."

"You still want me to stop by tonight?"

He looked down at the flattened cardboard for a minute. "Okay. Not sure why though... don't think we'll... Never mind... yeah, sure."

"See you at seven."

In spite of it all – his hurt, her marriage, his lack of faith in the subject altogether – Gator continued his tutorials with Katy Lemonade on the purposes and efficacy of herbs, supplements and essential oils.

She was now presenting a broad overview of detoxification and, in particular, golden seal's prodigious capabilities in the matter.

"Is that the same as that, that... *'golden root'* they always come in askin' for?" Gator interrupted, referring to the customers that lived over in Ford's Ford, who all had to pass through the sheriff's speed traps coming and going from Utinahica. Ford's Ford was – except for the clandestine Rooster – dry, so Sheriff Burstyn, or one of his deputies, always lay in wait for people coming home from Miss Her to harvest a few dollars and to make a point.

"Like the guy what asked if he *knew* he had ta drive through Burstyn's trap an' took some golden root could he get hammered an' pass the breath test? Or the blood test. 'specially if he'd-a smoked pot. I mean, he figured the drunk drivin' thing he could prob'ly handle, jus' pay off Burstyn an' promise ta drink at the Rooster next time, but he was scared a maybe Burstyn checkin' for weed in'is pee or in his blood if he jus'pissed his pants ta ditch it or somethin'."

"Yes it is. And, wow, that is every kinda fucked up. What'd ya *tell* him?"

"I jus' asked him if he *knew* what he's drivin through the trap couldn't he jus' *not* smoke pot that night."

"*People...* " she sighed, shaking her head, then exclaimed. "Hey, man... what did you mean by... when you started to say that you 'don't think we'll...' something... today? Didn't finish. What were you talking 'bout? Something 'bout... us."

Gator started to panic, not remembering what it was he had started to say earlier. Had he revealed something about his feelings?

Katy detected his confusion and added, "When I asked if you still wanted me to come over."

"*Ohhhh...* Oh. Yeah," he said, relieved. "No. I was talkin' about... the store," he explained. "I don' know... I hate ta say it, but... I don't know much longer... it's got."

"Ohhh, man. Don't say that."

"Well..."

"No... I know what you mean, man. I didn't want to say it... out loud... hex it... or even think it. But I... Man, I love our little store. Such a bummer... It's... it's all I've..." she stopped short and looked away.

"Things are jus'... changin'," Gator said. He looked at Katy, knitted his brow sadly and whispered, "*Changed*."

Katy dropped her head, "I know. I wish..." then paused. "Folks are... splitting. And I don't think the store can hold on with just the Adventists and the Mennonites."

"Yoders are cool," Gator offered.

"Yeah, they're really mellow, but all the freaks... they're all moving up north..."

"Just north or big 'N' North?"

"Does it matter?"

"Naw, I... I reckon not. Maybe I need ta kick up some dust myself."

Katy seemed as sad as she ever had but steeled up enough to scold Gator, "*You* never liked the hippies anyways."

"That... that ain't ex-*act*ly true," he said.

He knew what he had said before, that stupid thing about dogs, but, truth be told he didn't dislike hippies. In fact, he related to them as outsiders and as all potential criminals in the eyes of what they would call, "The Establishment," for which he himself had never had any use.

What he did not like about them was that they – Vernal Equinox in particular – challenged, ridiculed even, his own dreams, his goals, and essentially all of the works of his beloved objective field as corrupt, destructive, in opposition to Nature... A privileged few among the academics and creators were excused: the scientist's job was to know, to understand – purely – they said; the architect's even was to build anew, for shelter, and in the great soaring cathedrals and temples manifesting man's striving, reaching to god, they said; even the chemist extracted their drugs from the vegetable kingdom, they said; and with all would he wholeheartedly concur. BUT the *engineer*... They said his work was to, and only to, *defeat* Nature: to tear into the earth, to scrape away the soil, to blast the rock, they said; to pave the miles for roads that strangled the world, to dam all free-flowing rivers, they said. To make the low places high, the high places low, the crooked way straight. This was unfair, he said; the engineer's job was, at worst, to *harness* nature for the benefit of mankind, he said – the way the ones out at the defunct commune had harnessed that mule, he said; the Roman engineer brought the water from the mountains, leagues away, and their very name, *"ingeniator,"* was forged from words for "create" and "ingenious," he said; and bridges were beautiful, lofty temples in their own right, he said. And, anyway, hadn't all of mankind always done these things? Not just the engineer, but the carpenter, the mason – the artist and sculptor, so easily credited with lofty inspiration – even the simplest craftsman: all took the bending tree, the hunchbacked rock, colorful mineral, malleable clay, even the formless wind and water and straightened, planed, poured, turned, made to billow and drive... and thereby remade them all to things with empirical, exacting arithmetic qualities, for things we call "useful" or even "beautiful."

"But *no*..." Gator boiled, "*HE* says it is nature 'channeled...' 'withheld...' 'chained...' *'forced*...' 'Molested.' Really... *He*, of all people..."

Ah... He was a fucking hippie. What did he know?

"You still there?" Katy asked, pulling him from his dark absorption.

"They... make fun of... me." was all he could muster and the most perfectly honest thing he could say.

"Like that kid today?" she asked.

"Yeah... *Yeahhh*," he said, almost with revelation.

"They were just... joking around." Katy said, thoughtlessly, she soon realized.

Gator looked at her with disappointment, "Jus' a joke... Jokes... I don't like... *jokes*..." he said emotionlessly, then began to speak.

"Back in school... here... over ta Milton High... there'uz this girl, Betty Rose Howard, who... well, there had ta be somethin' wrong with'er. I guess. She jus' looked... old. Gray, thinnin' hair, wrinkles, Coke bottle horn-rimmed glasses, veiny hands. Looked like she was... sixty. Progeria or somethin'... I don't know. Nobody did... Her an' her family kept ta themselves... An'... man... wow... she didn't have *any* friends... at all. Always by herself. No one even... inter*acted* with'er. It was... Jesus... sad. Even the... mean girls didn't mess with her 'cause it was too... *heartless*... even for them. I'd talk ta her... well, *say* things ta her... sometime, or try... jus' say, 'hello'... but she was so shy or embarrassed or whatever from nobody ever talkin' ta her. I mean... sometime in class she'd... or at least she'd try ta, like, join in in a discussion, but... she was... paid no attention, like she wasn't there. *Man*... But... I reckon there's always lonely, outcast kids, an'... at least she didn't get picked on... really. I guess that ain't sayin' much... really...

"An' it always seemed... felt... like inside-a her was this... nice, 'regular' ... desperate ta jus' be a regular high school girl, but, ya know... trapped in this... *situation*... what, was jus'... damn... only gonna get worse. Anyways, loneliest..." he paused and took a deep breath, " '*Alone*-est' person I ever did see. Even in prison..."

Gator reflected for a moment.

"Then..."

He took another long breath,

"... there'uz this other kid, Chaz Bamhill... *'Bamm-Bamm.'* Family moved up from Jacksonville... for the mill company... city kid... He wore boots an' striped bell-bottoms an' a scarf an' swinged'is bangs outta'is eyes when he clicked down the hall or walked inta the classroom. Looked like Greg Brady or... no, like that kid on... *Scooby Doo*... One what drove the van. Oh yeah, an' all the girls thought he was *soooo dreamy* 'cause, get this, 'cause he was s'posed ta be in the next grade, but he was a dumbass an' failed, so he was held back, so all these chicks think he's all Bobby Sherman 'cause he's a '*older* man.' Big class crush... So, he worked all that shit. But, yeah, he's dumb as a bucket a doorknobs... fuckin'... nimrod, but full a himself. I mean, I hung around with him... sometime. But, hell, I mean, kids... ya know... I mean, like dogs, ya know? Just hang out with other ones. Ya know?"

He sounded apologetic.

"Yeah, sure, Gator," Katy comforted.

"His dad blew a bugle ta call him home at suppertime...

"So... this mornin'... it's home room... it's before the bell... he calls me an' Booger an' Rollins over an'... an' he shows us he's got a bag a rocks, an', an' ol' dog turds... bag a turds, see?... An' rocks... big fuckin' bag a shit an' rocks..."

Gator rubbed his chin vigorously and became perceptibly agitated, gesticulative.

"An' we ask'im, 'What the heck... What the heck with the bag a dog crap, Bamhill?' an' he's sayin' 'it's Valentine's day...' an' now he's got this heart-shaped box... Old Whitman candy box an'... an'

"'Well, I'm a-gonna put this dog-dirt an' rocks in this box an' give it ta Betty Rose!'

"My blood... jus'... runnin' cold...

"'For Valetnine's! HaHaHa... It'll be funny!'

"An' I'm, 'No, man! No. You can't do that, you *CAN'T* do this...' even dumbass cracker Donny Rollins... 'No man no...' an' Bamm-Bamm's... Bamm-Bamm, *really*...? You're *laughin'*? You're *laughin'*? Really?"

Katy saw that Gator was back there now, in it, not so much telling the story as reliving it out loud.

"'What? What? It's gonna be so funny...' Nooo, man... Somethin' terrible... set in motion... Somethin' terrible an'... irreversible, like... fallin' off a cliff... this *awful* thing I can't stop it... fallin' jus'... waitin' ta hit bottom... Booger's, 'Man, you can NOT do this shit!' 'No... No...' everybody's 'No' an' Bamm-Bamm he's laughin' an' loadin' up his box, I'm panickin'; somethin's gotta... gotta *stop* this. 'You can't do this, man... You can't do this...' Booger's walkin' in circles... Rollins's sittin' in his desk with his head in his hands...

"Betty Rose's walkin' in the door... now, it's like... like a train's comin' at me... can't get outta the way... Betty Rose... walkin' in the door... before the teacher gets there... I can't tell her... tell the teacher what ta make it stop... Betty Rose walkin' in the door... I'm in the cloakroom... Bamm-Bamm's up an' he's walkin' *at* her with his hand behind his back... walkin' up ta Betty Rose... grinnin' like a possum eatin' shit... there should be a gas leak... a explosion... somethin'... an' Betty Rose she's... stunned? Confused...? Why is he in front a her...? Terrified even, like she's gonna get killed an' he pulls his hand from behind his back..."

Gator stopped for a moment, then more slowly resumed his tale, shaking his head.

"Nope... It's too late... It's too late... can't be undone... It's too late... She's took the box, Yep, she took it... Now she's lookin' at this heart-shaped box an' looks at Bamm-Bamm an'... an' *gasps*... Little... *lliiiiittle* gasp a air, like she's about ta speak, but no words follow... " Gator's voice dropped and he made odd little pinching motions with his thumb and forefinger, like a little bird pecking, "Jus' keeps makin' these little wordless gasps.

"An'... she is the *happiest* person in the *whooole* world. Like nobody ever gets ta really be... Like it's like a *dream... dream* what she's dreamed ev'ry night. Like... a *secret* dream, *'That'* dream... Too fulla happiness, too crazy, so far away... Yeah, too painful what ta ever... admit... out loud... where it'd die in the light. Like, it'd be smothered... by the, like the... the pain a its... its... *never-ness*... only bearable alone in the dark a her room, her *cell,* where dreams could be... real... where dreams can be more'n what they are – jus' dreams – an' she dreams it every night. An' now... Now, *here it was*, real... Real real, alive, in the world, in *this* world... Real ta her poor, never acknowledged heart... Can you *imagine?* Can y-... ...An' she's hyperventilatin', an' smiles a smile, a real smile. Real... *joy* spreads over her face, maybe for the first time... makes her eyes sparkle, her papery skin crinkle 'round her big eyes with joy she ain't *never* known. She can't even speak, her heart so swole up in her throat. Bamm-Bamm smiles down ta her... down... like a... like a *prince*, but he's jus' tryin' ta keep from sputterin' out loud...

"She's lookin' back down ta the box, then up ta him, then back down an' she's... she's pullin' up the lid... pulling it open... Then... like the world cracked open... " Gator made a motion with his hands like breaking something violently apart, "Broke... It's too late... it's done...

"There's... what? Like, firecrackers... Black Cats... No... Rocks... It's rocks... rocks hittin' the floor... Right, right... clackin', cracklin'... Then the heart... falls... Now... What is... what is *that* sound? There's a *sound*... what *is* that sound?" He put his palms to the side of his head and bemoaned, "Hands pressed ta my ears an' it's *still* there." He dropped his hands and looked around. "Like the room... the buildin'... the whole world's in pain... Make it stop... the sound... Sound a... rippin' outta that... dream... Back here. The sound, the sound a her... wakin' *up*...

"An' that sound don't stop...

"Teacher come in... tryin' ta sort out what's goin' on...

"An' that sound don't stop...

"We sit in our desks starin'...

"An' that sound don't stop...

"Bamm-Bamm, standing there lookin' stupid, smilin' like, 'What? Why ain't folks laughin'?...'

"An' that sound don't stop...

"Principle come down, nurse come down, an' she... Betty-Rose never even left the room... jus' crumbled inta Joy Stubb's desk with the lid a that box... that heart... in 'er hand an' cried...

"An' that sound never stopped..."

He was silent for a moment again, gathering his senses. He shook his head slowly and went on,

"Then... then, maybe worst a all... Finally... Her ol' man come ta pick her up. This old dude, sad lookin' little man... some kinda worker, custodian kinda guy, kinda guy what wears a khaki uniform with his name on the shirt... 'Bud'... I mean... *'Bud,'* Jesus Christ...

"I mean, ya know... folks... most folks... jus' want their kids ta be happy an'... this poor bastard, he jus' wants his kid ta be... I know he looks at his little girl every day an'is heart breaks... jus' on every normal day... for his little girl that would never be... jus'... *wanted* his... his *little girl* ta be... regular... I mean... how little a thing ta want. But the biggest most impossible thing. Jus' his little girl ta be regular...an' happy. An' it was hard enough every day, an' it hurt him when she hurt... An' now... this... this, whatever it was that made... this... an' now... now here she is, this sobbin', humiliated, hurt little thing crushed by cruelty... An', man, you could see... his face... *was* a broken heart... "

He sat for a minute looking at the floor.

"Never saw her again...

"All for a... heart fulla shit...

"An' that sound ain't never stopped. Still..."

Gator sat silently.

Katy Lemonade sat for long while – waiting to make sure the story was over... That it was gone.

Then she went to where he sat, staring into space, and placed her arm around his head and held him tight to her breast.

"*the – weak – are – devoured – by – the – strong...*" Gator mumbled into her halter top.

She stroked his hair and whispered, "*Shhhhhhhh...* Hush... they'll inherit the earth. It's all cool."

She thought she felt him sob briefly and shake his head. But it might have been a laugh.

After another long silence she asked, "What happened to... Greg Brady?"

"Kicked his ass."

"*Hmmmmm...* Was that after...after you... after your...?"

"Woudn'ta mattered. He's a punk..."

"Ya know... I don't like jokes, those jokes, either but I don't like ass-kicking too."

"Ya gotta believe in it..." he said flatly to himself.

Katy stood quietly, then said, "I don't know what you're talking 'bout... now, but... ya know, you remember a lot of things. Stuff. Your brain holds a lotta... details." She absent-mindedly, gently, tousled his hair.

"Ughh... I don't know... Everybody remembers shit... An', memories... they get beat up, rusty, dented... We bang out the dents an' Bondo an' polish 'em, so they look like new... maybe even a little better'n when they rolled off the showroom floor... so maybe it ain't all the right details, ya know? But 'long as it's still the same model, I guess. Sometimes we jus' build a whole new car, though."

"Yeah. hahaha... Well, I get the idea most of what you remember is right on."

"Some shit I wish I... didn't have ta remember."

"Like that story? Things you remember, still feel, but try to hide from?"

"*Hide* from...? Nah, it's jus'... throwin' trash over the back fence so you don't have ta look at it."

Still cradling his head, she gave it a few quick but gentle jerks, "OK... 'grumpy,' same thing... I can tell you're a big softy... But, really, you've got... potential, man. You're smart, you could do something besides... the store. Mopping up and... *pretending* to sell vitamins... Something you dig, ya know, like that school thing."

"But Equinox says..."

"It's not 'bout what he thinks... He's not always... even... handed." She sat down across from him and looked him in the eye. "But you're on *your* path, man... your journey. You're a real smart cat... Find your own way."

"Thanks." Gator said with genuine gratitude for her concern regarding his well-being. It was something he was unaccustomed to.

"But, yeah, you got some chemicals in your head..." she added.

"*Excuse* me?" he barked, taken aback.

"You know, brain chemicals..."

"What? Why are you... goin' *there?*"

"No. I'm sorry," she reached out and touched his arm. "I meant memory molecules."

"*'Memory molecules'?*"

"Yeah. Memories are chemical..."

Gator groaned

"No, really! Memories are molecules... molecules we make for what we remember..."

"Jesus... So... Frank Bank. There's a chemical in my brain for Frank Bank? There's a Frank Bank molecule?"

"Why do you always do this! This stuff is important to me!"

"I'm sorry, it just sounds..."

"What do *you* think makes memories?"

"Good times?" he said, then began to sing,

>"Here's ta gooood friends,
>Tonight is kinda speciallll..."

"Stop! See... smarty pants, you don't even know... you just... you just 'know' *I'm* wrong!" She stood up as her voice began to quaver, "*You* always make fun of *me*... and it... it hurts... Gator... " She stopped, then, barely audible, she looked to the floor and muttered like a hurt child, "...said you don't like jokes..."

Her hurt, her fragile demeanor, her sense of betrayal after showing him such warmth and communion shook Gator and filled him with remorse and a contrition he desperately needed to express.

But he did not know how. He had never known how to make things right.

So he just said, "Sorry," because for him that one word contained everything, the sum, the completeness, the alpha and the omega of all he felt – sorrow – then ham-handedly went to flattery.

"Well, you got potential too. You're smart. You know things. Hell, ya know more'n I do about everything in the store. I mean, how come *you* ain't the vitamin guy?"

"'Cause I'm 'just' a chick... You know how y'all are about all *that!*"

"*I'm* not. I just asked why ya weren't doin' the vitamin guy!"

She snorted and, blushing, he grappled to clarify himself, " ...I mean, doin' the vitamin thing... weren't the... doin' the vitamin... person... *thing.*"

"Yeah... Okay. Mellow out, man. It's all cool. It's all cool."

"I jus' think you're too good to stay trapped in this burgh," he went on still trying to salvage the moment.

"Don't know I could scratch up that kinda bread... to move somewhere... better." She looked up suddenly, as if in revelation and chirped, "OH! Yeah! And I'm married! HA! Got an old man. Hahahaha. Oh, man... Ha.... heh... ...ahem. Uh... Okay... well, I reckon I oughta... get truckin'."

Gator walked Katy to the porch then down the stairs where he said, "Uh oh... Goin' down stairs... look out... we're losin' our potential."

"Is that a joke?" Katy sighed.

"Yeahhh, I reckon, maybe..."

She stopped upon reaching the yard and said, "You don't like jokes..."

She turned to face him and stood close, looking at him as if expecting something.

They looked at each other.

He didn't have whatever it was.

She turned to stroll off towards her car in the yard.

He stayed at the bottom of the steps and called back, "Yeah, well... Nobody likes that one... " and thought "What the hell does *that* mean?" then called out, again, "Okay... *via con dios!*"

I spite of the jolly face he was putting on now and the pleasure he found in watching her swish away Gator was still unsettled from remembering Betty Rose and still stinging from Katy's rebuke and the hurt she felt and his own hurt which he denied via his assholeness. He thought about it and her and if he was being mean – intentionally – because she was with that *other* asshole.

"That'd be uncool," he thought. "I gotta plow through... an'... an' be cool with all this. With her... *To* her."

Then he thought, "Damn, I suck. Maybe, maybe it's for the best," he thought. "Way things are... For her."

Katy stopped at the Volkswagen, fumbling for her keys in her burlap shoulder sack and he looked at her and his mind turned on him. Maybe, maybe, he thought, maybe he *envied* her. She *could* turn him away... get away. Escape from him. "I can't, I'm *stuck*... Without me, there is no me," he lamented. "I'm like my own evil twin. Siamese evil twin..."

He realized they weren't even together and here he was trying to give her reasons to break up with him... But, still, he knew how he felt and knew that he had allowed her closer than anyone – probably than anyone ever – and surely that was why he had just told her one of the things he never talked about to anybody: one of the few things that, inexplicably, he felt, made him emotional. There was that thing and how his brother had died trapped in an old refrigerator.

"Trash over the back fence..."

The bug sputtered to a start. Katy backed it up then began to putt off down towards the drive: towards the twin's house.

That thought made him tense up momentarily, but he shook it off and thought, "An', man... she smelled good up close... sweat an' sandalwood..."

The VW's brake lights flashed on and it lurched to a stop. Without poking her head out the window she called out, loudly, "...Who's *Frank Bank?*"

***

JD Hollingsworth

June 18, 1977

Gator had mysteriously and atypically been absent from the end of Mill Spring Road for nigh on a week. When he returned that Saturday afternoon it was hot.

Marie, sitting in the shade of her porch, called to him as he exited the Capri.

He held his hand to his forehead and squinted to spot her among the nature's floristry, sagging from the persistent drought, all around her veranda.

"Gater!" she called again and spat a gob of snuff juice on the roses: she said it killed the aphids, though she called them something he'd never heard before, "neat o' th' pismire," or something.

"You a-funeralize yer ma?" she yelled hoarsely.

In fact, Gator had funeralized his mother only a few days earlier. Arlene had fallen ill the week before and he had taken her to the hospital in Warner Robins where she shortly passed on from complications of congestive heart failure. The Toomey brothers painted her face, and the Reverend Pine said solemn, generic, words over her grave, which Willie Milton shoveled dirt in atop her and wiped off the small family stone into which her final day awaited to be chiseled. Gator got stoned and went fishing from the remains of the old Okgatalatchee Bridge.

"Yes, I did... Thanks for askin'."

"Arlene a-laid under alongst ta yer pappy out ta th' Macedonia boneyard?"

"Yes..."

"What ta a-come a ol' Skeeve?" she asked with slight, but apparent, disdain.

Gator squinted and sucked on a tooth, wondering, "how does she know any of... " then could only respond, "Not my problem..."

"Ah's a-sorry Gater, hopes what ya ain't a-got th' morbs too greatly."

"I'm… Okay. Thanks, Marie."

"Death a-come a-knockin' by 'is own reck'nin. N'er a minute later."

"Yeah… I reckon. Anyways, I'm kinda wiped out, Marie. Gonna go cop some Zs…"

"AHHH…HAhahahahaha!" she cachinnated then began to buzz,

"zzzzzzzzz zzzzz bzzz bzzz bzzzz bzzz bzzz bzzzz bzzzzzzzzz"

and then to sing… and to buzz.

"Mister San'man, brang me a dream bzzz bzzzz bzzzz bzzzzzzzzzz

Make'im th' cutest what I ever seed bzzz bzzzz bzzzz bzzzzzzzzzz

Give'im two lips a-like roses 'n' clover

Tell'im 'is lonesome nights is over"

Gator climbed the stairs to his house swatting at the swarm of pestering words.

"HAHAHA! Zzzzzzz zzzzzzzzzz bzzzzz zzzzzzzzz HA HA hahahaha!

Please a-turn on yer magik beeeeeee-"

The door slammed behind him.

He could still hear her cackling and buzzing outside.

"Man, she is *full* a beans today… Goddamn, now I ain't never gonna get ta sleep!"

Fourteen hours later Gator awoke wanting a drink.

It had been a stressful week, but it was Sunday and the refrigerator was empty so he was going to have to drive over to Ford's Ford to the bootlegger, who was also the sheriff thereabouts.

Gator knew the routine: pull into the lot of the body shop and drive around back to the window where, sometimes the sheriff, but usually ruddy-faced Mrs. Burstyn would hand out a six pack or a case of whatever she had a mind to. No words were exchanged: only cash. If you didn't know what it cost you were a stranger, unwelcome and had best get.

But it appeared lifeless today.

He drove slowly up the street towards the garage, hunched down and leering as he evaluated the scene. Two boys rode bicycles listlessly around in the blazing, dusty road tracing a lazy, unchanging circle in the dirt: each the pursued and the pursuer, they revolved ceaselessly in opposition, like figures on some medieval German tower clock. Gator stopped in front of the garage looking for signs of activity and the boys expanded their orbit to lasso the Capri.

"Y'all lookin' fer th'bootlegger?" the orbiting boy closest to the car called out as he passed without altering his path.

"Yeah..."

"Gone fishin," the other half of the pair replied when in perigee to the vehicle.

"*Both?* Ol' lady Burstyn too? She ain't never gone..." he asked, craning his head out the window as if to somehow bring forth an attendant by his efforts.

"Annivers'ry," whichever boy was nearest in circumgyration answered.

"Nabbit! What a crap day!" he complained. "Now I gotta go ta the Rooster..."

Gator mopped his brow and made a three-point turn from the garage lot through a break in the juvenile orrery's movement and headed back down Ford Street towards the woods. He looked in the rear view and watched the binary boys lethargically looping, over and over, and imagined them continuing until their orbits decayed and they crashed into one another at their barycenter in the middle of that scorching red dirt road. Then he headed deep into the forest.

Miles on through the woods on the far side of Ford County was the Red Rooster. The Rooster was not really a thing, because it wasn't legal, but it was a thing because it had a name. It was not really a roadhouse because it wasn't on the road or in a house, but it was in a barn and at the end of a drive. No one knew about the Rooster, but everybody did and it was always packed with folks who would swear they had never set foot there: even to one another. And for every one there was an other: for, owned by the – some might say, progressive – sheriff of Ford County, the Rooster welcomed all. If church was the most segregated hour of the week, the Red Rooster was the most integrated continuum and Sherriff Burstyn provided every need – drinking, gambling, cockfights, battles royale, and whores – for every needy soul, be they "black, white, red, yeller, er polky-dotted," as he would say, "'cause alla them's money is green."

Gator had planned to just grab a six-pack and head back to Utinahica but long after sundown he found himself still at the bar spending the money he had made on the outcome of the bare-knuckles bout, liberally distributing the wealth to strangers and friends alike.

Gator's childhood friends Hairston and Booger and Booger's common-law wife Becky-Lynn had also chosen to spend this sweltering Sunday taking advantage of the Rooster's air-conditioning,

111

activities, and, as it turned out, Gator's winnings. A portion of those winnings had also been used to purchase a baggie of the sheriff's finest seized evidence and now, nearing the witching hour, Booger and Gator were still babbling on under its predictable influence.

"Fate's bullshit man... I... I am a *free* motherfucker. God an' Jefferson gimme a choice 'bout what... 'bout what I does," Booger philosophized, nursing his Coke.

"Man, ain't fate what I'm talkin' about..." Gator corrected." S'bout whether ya can say somethin' coulda happened if... somethin' else didn't... or did..."

"That's that's... yeah.... No. What?" Booger said, scratching his head.

"Ya... ya don't get ta work offa what didn't happen for what coulda happened after... ya know, *compadre*? Ya know, 'if only' shit... future contingents..." Gator rambled. "Like, like folks think like, 'Oh, man, if Matthews'd a got a single instead-a a ground out an' then when Montañez come up next and had a hit that homer he did, well shit, he'd a hit in two runs, 'stead a one, an' won the game in the ninth... blah blah, 'stead a us losin'... again.' But, see, e-ver-y-thing woulda changed after that single... the single what he ain't got in the firs' reality... Woulda set up a whole diff'rent set a... a... situation. Everything'd be altered, *amigo*... Montañez wouldn'ta got the same pitch, at the same time... made the same swing, connected the same way... All be diff'rent... Montañez'd never a got that homer... see? Ya'd jus' have Matthews on first... An' be a run behind."

"Wow.... Yeahhh... " Booger nodded, momentarily impressed, then countered, "But... Well, he mighta had a-gotten *a* home run... Maybe not *THAT* home run, but he coulda gotten *a* home run. Diff'rnt home run. Maybe ya don't never really get a *second* chance but ya get a whole new, *diff'rent,* chance,"

"Tha's a... tha's a 'nother whole diff'rent ball a wax... there... But, yeah, ya don't *get* no secon' chances in real life neither. That is, not a shot at the same actual, *sing-u-lar* event. Know what I mean? I mean, ya get three pitches, but ya don't get th'actual same pitch again... Ya don't walk in the same stream twice, ya know?"

"Shit, I walk in Rangle's Branch alla time lookin' fer turtles..." Booger objected.

"Turtles... for what?"

"I like 'em."

"Yeah turtles are cool... but what was ... somethin'... ya still can't even *say* a thing what occurred... ...Ya mean, for *eatin'*?"

"What?"

"Turtles."

"No."

"OK... so somethin' about somethin' after woulda happened if a thing ya wanted ta happen had happened... *Man*..." Gator tried to regain his derailed train of thought.

There was a long stoned pause.

"What?" Booger asked as if just arriving at the conversation after draining the rest of his cola.

"I don't know what we're talkin' about the same shit no more..." Gator said soberly.

Becky-Lynn, eyes closed with her drunken head lolling around, chin in hand, loudly commanded, "Gawd, y'all shut up..."

Hairston, laying face down on the bar, mumbled, "Need ta go *hooome*," and Booger determined it was time to get out. "Jus' let me get another Coke ta stay awake."

A big potbellied and shirtless country boy staggered up to where they sat, all sloppy arms and slappy hands all over Booger as he arrived, and bellowed, "Hey, Boog! Boog, Boog... Hey, Boog..."

"What it is, my man?" the affable Booger, greeted the big hands-y man.

"Hey Boog. Hey... Hey, listen... Boog... listen... How come... How come Dolly Parton's feet'r so small?"

"I dunno Bird Dog, why?"

"'Cause, 'cause, 'cause they... ain't-never-had-no-*SUN*light... HAR HAR harharhar..."

"Ha, yeah, that's a good one there, Dog."

"Ya... ya get it? Ya get it . Boog? Ya know... 'cause... 'cause..."

"Yeah... she's got a big chest. An' feet need sunlight... I reckon'... Hey, could I get another Coke?"

"Chest?"

"Gawd, y'all shut up..." Becky-Lynn, called, half-conscious, from her chin.

The Coke arrived. Booger went for cash in his pocket but Gator said, "Got it," and waved his finger around somehow indicating to the bartender that it was on his now mostly diminished tab.

"Alright, my man," Booger thanked.

The big shirtless hayseed staggered around in place, looked Gator up and down and said, "Whatta *you* know?"

"Not much, *muchacho*..."

Booger could see Gator's brain starting to misfire and interrupted, "Hey, he knows... what was it...? Oh, yeah, like... baseball an' shit."

113

"Base-*ballll?*" the big man questioned. "Hell, I don't know no... base-*ballll* jokes. Tell me one a... one a yer base-*ballll* jokes..."

"I don't think..." Booger began, but Gator interrupted to say, "Okay, so there are these... these three umpires, see, an' somebody asks 'em ta tell how they call balls an'... an' strikes, an' the first one, he says," Gator adopted an officious tone, "'Well, if the ball passes over the... over the plate an' it's b'tween the batter's armpits ta the top a his... his knees when it crosses, it's a strike... otherwise it's a ball...'"

The big farm boy swayed like tree in a high wind, blinking and trying to pay attention...

"An' the second umpire, he says, 'if they're balls I call 'em balls, an' if they're strikes I call 'em, strikes.'"

The big man burped.

"So the last umpire, so he says..." Gator went to a tough guy voice, "'Dey ain't *nothin'* 'til I calls 'em!' *haw*hawhaw!"

"Huh?" the man grunted, then, "Har Har harhar har... Tha's a a good base-*ball* joke..." then vomited and slouched off.

"More of a... a 'physics' joke, I reckon..." Gator called after him.

"Gawd, y'all shut up..."

"Hoooommmme," Hairston mumbled to the bar.

"Alright man," Booger said, "gotta get th'ol'lady and this dude ta home."

Gator helped deposit Hairston on the back seat and load Becky-Lynn in the front of Booger's Camaro and tried to get her to move her arm to the side when he fastened the belt.

As Booger was opening the door to the Z28 Gator warned, "Oh wait, man, don't go back by the County Road... Burstyn's got a... a trap or roadblock, or..."

"S'okay... I'm sober."

"I know, but don't matter... wouldn't chance it with *that* guy," and Gator nodded over to where Burstyn – there celebrating his anniversary with his wife – stood chewing on a cigar and braying like a jackass at the Dolly Parton joke. "Go back by the back way, out by the Fitzgerald road... 'round by my place."

"Okay, thanks for the tip my man, I reckon things coulda gone bad... never know."

They gave a soul brother handshake and Gator lit a cigarette. The Camaro door closed with a solid, satisfying "thunk," roared on then rumbled as Booger started towards the dirt drive. He stopped and put his head out.

"There *are* second chances..." he called back. "You got one, brother." He winked and drove on.

Gator thought that it seemed like he had only got a second chance to strike out, but called back, "Night y'all."

"Gawd, y'all shut up..."

As he neared Mill Stream Road Gator was still stoned and wondering, "I wonder... I wonder'f that molecule'd be the *same* molecule for everyone what thought a... " when he saw sparkles of silver and red twinkling like stars in the darkness of the road just beyond the turnoff. He drove on a little further, past his drive, then slammed on his brakes when he saw that the glittering lights were reflecting from shattered glass and taillight lenses scattered over the road. Beyond, in the headlights, Booger's Z28 lay upside down and sideways in the road.

Gator jumped from his car, ran a few steps, then stopped in a panic. The steam escaping from the muscle car's punctured radiator hissed like a snake and the squeaking of the wheel that was even now still spinning seemed to mock him like the laughing of a hyena. He drew a deep breath and ran a few more steps. He stopped again. He shuffled his feet in a dance of indecision, then crouched down, took a breath and hopped sideways like a monkey to the Chevy where his reluctance to look more closely had him bobbing his head like a chicken as he steeled his nerve to peer inside. He held his breath as if about to dive beneath the water, ducked his head down and looked through the window. In the beam of his headlights, he saw Becky-Lynn, still held to her seat by the safety belt, hanging upside down, staring with a look, not of terror or peace or even puzzlement, but only of when-will-this-ever-end boredom. Her arms bent over her head like a ballerina's. The horizontal offset of her neck told him she would never again be bothered with unwelcome conversation.

Through the car he could see that the driver's door was wide open.

He stood quickly, squeezed his mouth in his hand, then looked around. Near the far edge of the road, half in the ditch, he saw what was left of Hairston. Fortunately he did not have the chance to look long because he heard something from the other side of the road and scuttled across the median to find Booger, gasping and trying to raise a hand.

Gator squatted down and, ignorant of any useful action to take, merely gave Booger a futile "I'm sorry" look and waved his open hands indecisively around him, finally closing them into fists, tight with frustration.

Booger opened and closed his mouth like a landed bass, trying to speak through the blood. Gator turned his ear towards him and dropped his head closer.

"Another... ...swing..." gurgled up and Gator turned his eyes back to Booger's only to see his look of longing melt away to share Becky-Lynn's ennui.

Gator shot to his feet and stepped back. "Did he really *say* that??" His arms rigid at his sides, fists clenched again in frustration, he hyperventilated then began to... scream, groan, laugh, bray... to vent some strange hybrid sound that bubbled up from the cauldron within, stewing with everything he felt, everything he denied, everything he held in: panic, despair, helplessness, loss, the fantasy of miracles, the reality of no, the fright of a lost and abandoned child...

"ahhhhhh
ahhhhhhh
ahhhhhhhh
ahhhhhhhhh
ahhhhhhhhhh
ahhhhhhhhhhhhhhhhhhhh"

What had caused this? Out here? There was no other car. There were no other cars – no traffic – at all, no sign of an impact... There was no dangerous curve... Booger didn't even drink. But here was his car – upside down – on the centerline.

There had to have been something in the road. A deer... a...

Then, over his own guttural utterances he heard something.

Somewhere, back in the woods, a cry, stranger than his own arose and grew louder, lingered, then dropped away. Far back in the forest, something, out there beyond the end of his road, way back beyond the twins' hornet-ruled shack – but still not far enough away for Gator – some kind of... animal... bellowed a deep, throaty moan filled with menace and misery that echoed through the pines.

Though already long standing in a patch of corpses, now, for the first time, the hair on his neck stood on end.

The cry wailed through once more and Gator stopped breathing. He waited and waited, frozen; only abruptly jerking with a start from the occasional knocks of the cooling engine and hisses of its fluids dripping onto parts still hot.

He remembered to breathe, but silently, and was now filled with more panic in this cumulative nightmare: What he was to do? Now? How?

Should he make a call? How? He couldn't just leave... *them*. Besides, someone had to stay, to make sure no others happened unawares upon, were sacrificed to, this hazard of the dead waiting like some haunted iceberg in the darkness to send them to their doom. He would have to send someone else: some wayfarer he saved from this gruesome fate.

Until then he had to stay: he had to watch the road.

"Yes... the road..."

Gator turned on his blinker, thinking it would somehow help, and waited terrified, sad, alone. At last a truck came along with an old farmer: a farmer, but a Korean War vet and one ready to do his duty. He spun the old Power Wagon around in the road and tore off for help. Now all Gator had to do was to wait and to watch.

He glanced back at the scene of carnage and in the light thought he saw movement in the car. He was sure he must be wrong but, still, he once more steeled himself and ran to the Camaro crouched and looked in the window. Becky-Lynn hanged there. Cold, stiff, still bored. He stood and looked both ways down the road hoping the police or whoever it was might be seen coming, but time passes slowly tending the dead and he knew that nowhere near enough time had passed for help to arrive.

The wind picked up and the tips of the trees began to wave way up high and to whisper. Once more he thought he heard the lonely haunting bellowing in the woods but told himself it was only the wind and for the next hour stood among the dead and watched; but not the road, not his friends, just watched into the blackness beyond the road where there was, he hoped, nothing.

Tow trucks are always the first and Bubb McLellan arrived with his hook and chain wrecker. The sheriff arrived soon after just to have a look, and the Toomeys arrived later with the town's only ambulance, but all there were beyond help, so Charles Hairston, Beauregard Lee "Booger" de La Fontaine, and Clarissa Becky-Lynn Puckett were delivered to the Toomey's facilities in town.

Gator drove slowly up Mill Spring Road, delaying his arrival at home where he would have to lay in his house alone in the dark and remember what had happened and what he had seen and what he had heard. He parked and sat for another moment then got out. Only the crickets were chirping tonight and there was no light or sign of life from any of the houses.

But he knew she was there. Sitting in the dark.

He stood in the yard and waited.

Frankenstein's Paradox

The crickets stopped chirping.
Marie began to sing from the shadows.

Their soul's a-been called by the Master
They a-died in a craysh on the way
An' I heard the groans a the dyin'
But, I din't a-hear nobody a-pray.
I din't a-hear no-bodeeee pray, dear brother
I din't a-hear nobody a-pray
I heard th' craysh on th' highhh-wayyy
But, I din't a-hear noooo-
-bo-
-deeeeee

a-prayyyyyyyyyyyyyyyyyyyy

The crickets chirped again.

Gator fell to his knees.

***

VI

JD Hollingsworth

June 27th

Katy Lemonade stared at the Health Hole's front window, festooned with construction paper notices for specials and clearance sales. But she wasn't looking at them. Her hands gripped tight the handle of the flyswatter and her fingers tensed, rolled and worked its twisted wire. Her eyes scanned the window's perimeter, its frame, the wide, dusty sill at its bottom. She was looking for something to swat, to kill, but, frustratingly, there was either no vermin presently in the place or the perpetually cranked air conditioning had slowed them to imperceptibly inactive, thwarting her blood lust.

F.T. Arbuthnot from the welding shop across the street came in and wandered aimlessly about the store. Katy turned around to monitor the unusual visitor's movements while still maintaining her vigilance for some arthropod, miscreant or knave worthy of smite. Her eyes darted about then, below the register, in the junk box, she caught sight of the old PVC "flute" Vernal Equinox had presented her upon their first meeting. She looked at it for a moment then viciously slapped at the tuneless polymer tube.

Arbuthnot lumbered his six foot six frame up to the counter and, with the quiet, hat-in-hand manner that was his nature, interrupted her chastisement to politely query, "'Scuse me Miss... Miss Lemonade is it? I ain't never been in hyere afore, an' I do apologize... shoulda oughta been more neighborly but, I hyeard somewheres what y'all... y'all makes a cup a coffee hyere. I hates ta ask but the Bunn's busted down ta Stricklan's an' well... I..."

"Ohhh!" she exclaimed, "No, no this makes me so...!" and came from behind the counter, dropping her scourge, to scurry to the back corner while continuing to enthusiastically effuse, "I would *love* to make you some coffee... but it'll be different! Really strong!"

"I'd sure be obliged, Miss Lemonade."

"No, Katy... it's Katy. So glad you came in!" and she began to fuss with the apparatus.

Arbuthnot pointed, "I seen this machine hyere, an', well, I wondered if'n this were a coffee pot a some sorts, but I weren't sure... thought maybe it... somethin' ta do with the 'frigerator or the water... Anyways, I don't mess with 'quipmant what ain't mine."

"No, man, you shouldn't...' she cautioned as the machine gurgled and sputtered. "You can't... *verrrry* specialized!"

The device completed its business and she handed Arbuthnot the little white porcelain cup of dribblings. The big welder looked at the tiny cup in his massive mitt, at Katy, at the cup and once again to Katy. She smiled up at him. He smiled back with the sort of tender pity the kindhearted might express encountering a street waif selling pencils. He crossed to the "café" where he lowered all of his three hundred twenty pounds onto one of the frail wire chairs at the little round table and nestled. Looking as he always did, sooty and disheveled, as if he had just walked out of an explosion, his Brobdingnagian frame in the tiny ice cream chair with the little twisted wire heart on its back, and his Lilliputian cup, which he could only hold by two fingers and therefore not help but extend his pinkie, he sat straight-backed like a giant at a child's tea party, genteelly sipping, occasionally glancing to Katy's unfailing and expectant gaze to raise his eyebrows, grin and gently nod in polite approval.

It was sweet, charming: kind. It was the decent gesture of a gracious man and made the sad Katy Lemonade smile.

Meanwhile, in the chilled and funky service space behind the reach-in cooler cases in the back Gator grouchily busied himself throwing out the old, spoiled cheese.

"Don' get it, man... " he grumbled, "they age this shit in caves for fuckin' months, but a week in this damn place an' everything grows a fuckin' blue beard."

To be honest, it was more than a week. As with everything else, few people came in to buy cheese anymore. Most of the town had never really warmed up to the Health Hole and all of the hippies had either been beaten up, left of their own free will, or were Vernal Equinox. Everything was going bad: spoiled. Which is why what he was really thinking was about all of the little actions in life – his in particular – that lead to disaster. All of the what-ifs that had piled up like sediment behind a dam, clogging the works... leaving him feeling powerless.

Could the thirty seconds it took to tell the umpire joke have altered events just enough so that... ? What if he had just not wanted a drink that Sunday? What if the sheriff had been wed on a different date, if he hadn't quit the roofing job, hadn't beaten that guy on the logging crew half to death for driving a nail through a snapping turtle's shell... What if he hadn't drowned...?

Life and all of the death outside the pen was so... unpredictable.

"What if a ketchup bottle had fallen out of a window on the other side of the world ten years before... or if one *had*, what if it hadn't?" he thought. "Damn... it's everything."

He stood up, stared ahead and said out loud, "If Betty Rose'd had a little a that fat kid's moxie..."

"Who mocks you?" Gator heard from behind in a voice he recognized and his pulse quickened. He turned to the cooler door and said, "Speakin' a Bluebeards..."

"You are *still* so full of negativity and toxins," the unkempt silhouette declared. "Get some black salve... it will draw out the poison."

"Man, if bullshit was knowledge you'd be a real well-informed person..." Gator stated with unusual authority. "You're a great source a... ignormation, We didn't *all* just bounce offa the turnip truck, ya know?"

Vernal looked through the cooler glass into the store, then back to Gator and smirked, "Most of you did... Especially you. You gotta get up pretty early in the morning to best me... *All* you hayseeds."

Gator found Equinox's breaking character and uncharacteristic honesty jarring and in the isolation of the cooler's back room and its opportunity to speak freely he responded in kind, "Yeah, well, you best watch your ass motherfucker 'cause I sleep till noon an' I still know exactly what *you're* full of... an' what you're up to."

Vernal eyed Gator up and down with slit-eyed arrogance and languidly sneered, "Good luck convincing anybody... *muth-ah fuck-ahhhh*."

Just then Katy appeared in the doorway behind Equinox and over his shoulder asked, with a tinge of suspicion, "What are you dudes up to?"

"Just keeping cool m'love... " Vernal replied without turning around. "Beating the heat."

Gator *was* keeping cool. Disturbed by recent occurrences, and perceiving what he saw to be the unfortunate and unintended consequences of what seemed like his every action, he was losing the will to engage in further verbal combat with Vernal and attempted to back down.

"It's all cool," he simply said.

He might bring ruin to himself a thousand ways, but not to her by tempting fate again.

"Allll cool." Vernal concurred.

Vernal was back to being himself – or back to being in character. But, regardless, Equinox's reveal was unnecessary: Gator already knew. There was so much of who he really was that was always obvious to him. Even if Gator had not felt it from the beginning, it had become perfectly visible by the angel of her presence that shone through it all – as it shone now as she stood behind him. Katy's light: the pure light of her being that betrayed Vernal's. It was like candling an egg and Gator could see the twisted, grotesque thing that squirmed within.

Still, even when Equinox went on, "But we should leave him here with his garbage... He needs to throw out more of his old, rotten foulness... All of it!" and kicked at the stock around Gator's feet. Gator closed his eyes and visualized fallen shelving, he would not engage. For her.

"Right *sweeeetummmmms?*" Vernal ingratiatingly smarmed.

Katy huffed, "Goddammit Vern..." not with anger, but disgust.

"But what would be left?" Equinox chortled, raising his hands in mock perplexity, then turned to reach out and muss Katy's hair with his knuckles in ostensible playfulness but with manifest malice.

She pushed him away and stomped back to the store.

"Just joking around!" he called out to the room then turned back to Gator, glanced to the floor and said, "You got a mess to clean up," then left the cooler.

Gator looked through the cooler's glass doors to watch Vernal leave the store then looked down to a loose flat of Yoder Farms organic grade A eggs at his feet from which a viscous yellow pseudopodium crept.

"Egg..." he droned in dull amazement.

"Yeah... I do."

Gator got out of his car in the yard, pausing to retrieve the rear-view mirror that had fallen off when he slammed the door. He tossed it in the open window then stopped to admire the flaming red, yellow, and violet sunset that owned half the early evening sky. It was glorious and still bright enough that he could see Marie sitting on her porch puffing on a corn cob pipe perched between her and the end of a yard of Old Briar.

He thought it actually smelled pretty good. But he had enough bad habits.

JD Hollingsworth

The chorus of spring peepers – hundreds... thousands – in the trees had transformed the canopy for acres around into a living Mormon tabernacle and its resident choir chirped and jingled a rhythmic, pulsating choral that sounded mechanical, almost electronically synthesized.

"Man, those... freakin' frogs are goin' bonkers!" Gator exclaimed, keeping his language free from his usual profanities, which he had learned, the hard way, Marie disdained.

"*Rain crows...*" she called back "Ha! Tetched as a herd a doodlebugs!"

"Sounds like a... a flyin' saucer," he opined.

"No, it don't..."

"...Okay, then ... Oh... Speakin' of... I heard somethin' in the woods... other night. Strange... animal cry... Woods... back over behind the knuckleheads' place... Think maybe a... a coyote?"

"No ky-yotes. No ky-yotes, ner bears, ner buf'lo 'roun' here... many a moon. Pr'bly a wild cat. Spec'ally one what be in love. Sprang dry, but still sprang."

"Yeah, sure... You're prob'ly right. Sure... a cat... a *bob*cat."

Gator yawned and joked, "Damn, is it tomorrow yet? Or is this day... is it still today... or is it over?"

"Hour be close at hand."

"... *Al*-right."

"Lightnin' bugs a-looks like 'em though."

"... What?"

"*HA*hahahahahaha!" Marie cackled like a madwoman.

"... Okay... Well, goin' in... Gettin' dark."

"Lord says, 'night cometh... when no man can work.'"

"Yeah... Okay... Well, good night, Marie."

"Night, Gater."

***

VII

JD Hollingsworth

July 4, 1977

peep peep peep   deedle deedle deedle   peep peep peep
peep peep peep   deedle deedle deedle   peep peep peep

"...*mur*der that fuckin' bird..." Gator mumbled as he zipped up his pants at the toilet.

The morning light, even filtered through the honeysuckle enshrouding his rear porch and windows, was bright, yet the manic rapping on the roof, like the meterless finger drumming of a distracted person, alerted him that it was raining.

He looked in the mirror and saw his face, slack-jawed and green in the gills. He laughed that this could possibly be the creature to carry her away to the safety of his black lagoon.

Gator stood on the porch smoking and waiting for the sun shower to pass over before heading out to work. It was the first rain anyone had seen in two months or more. The dirt road was hard and dry and the rain rolled off in dust-covered globules and rivulets as if off of a freshly waxed car. But it did smell like wet rock and right now that was good.

Still, there was not a cloud in the sky to block the sun.

Water wound down the rain chain Gator had hung in his gutter's vacant hopper in lieu of a downspout. He followed its path to the ground where it twinkled off a flat rock then ran off to a pool accumulating around a big clump of mint by one of the brick piers. Like a big silver eyeball, the puddle winked at him with every drip from the leaky open eves and rafter tails and between each wink, there in the puddle, he again saw his own face looking back up at him from over the railing. He was scowling, tense. It annoyed him. He looked away.

Across the road through the sparkling sunshine he saw the brothers hurl some liquid of their own at the vexing nest then immediately begin to jump around and run away down the road.

He was impatient to get to work because Katy Lemonade had asked if he would help her with his car and Gator thought, assumed, hoped, it was to escape the wigwam of Equinox. Which was good for many reasons, one of which was that Gator did not know how much longer, even without direct observed proof of physical abuse he could go without destroying the duplicitous peacenik that had destroyed Katy's spirit.

"Devil's a-beatin' 'is wahf!"

Gator looked over to the words from Marie's porch through the rain that shimmered in the sun like tinsel on a Christmas tree.

Since that frozen day months before, he could still barely allow himself to look at her house closely for fear that he might see... something, peeking from behind one of the perpetually drawn, heavy Victorian curtains. But now he smiled and waved with his smoke.

"Devil..." Marie called out again, removing the corn cob pipe she had turned upside town to keep from being snuffed out by the falling drops. *"He's a-beatin' 'is wahf!"* and made a vague gesture to the weeping world beyond, and Pungo the Second sneezed in agreement.

"Yeah..." Gator concurred with a long waft of exhaled Camel. "Yeah, he is."

Gator went ahead and trotted out into the bright sunshine and pouring rain to head on to work. He drove down the dirt drive still shedding the rain as if it were waterproofed, when one of the soaking twins waved him down. Gator rolled down his window and began, "Need ta get ta work, dudes, right n-*OWOWahuahh!* – Jesus *fuck*, man! Your *face!*"

The wet face of whichever twin had stuck it in the window was gruesomely swollen up from stings.

"*Damn*, man, you look like... Frazier after Manila," Gator complained.

"Whu'? ...Hey bro," the twin blathered on, oblivious, "we tried a-shootin' strikes anywheres matches from th'air gun at 'em 'ere warsps but it di'n't work..."

"Really? .:.That's what you wanted?"

"Naw... Ya doin' fer th' fourth?" he said, getting to the point.

"Probably goin' ta Miss Her."

"We gots a shit ton a bottle rockets an' nigger chasers an'..."

"Ahhhhh ugh... No. Yeah, I gotta go." Gator rolled up the window against the fading rain and the gargoyle-ish twin and drove on, hoping that the wasps prevailed.

Along the way to work, Gator realized that he had been stung after rolling down his window: fraternizing with the enemy. He walked into the Health Hole rubbing his arm and immediately asked Katy, standing at her usual post behind the register, what it was she had wanted. She would not make eye contact and just kept saying to forget it, that she had changed her mind. She was vehement but kept her voice low. He began to feel angry then heard from back in the store, "Rosy *Frank*-lin, my friend!"

Gator turned to see Vernal Equinox "shopping" and grazing in the bulk bins.

"How are you, bright this early morn?" Equinox asked with great smarm and a mouthful of yogurt pretzels.

Gator just rubbed his arm and looked at Equinox then at Katy who stood looking down at her hands on the counter.

Equinox saw Gator absent-mindedly worrying the spot on his arm and lied, "Ohh, I know this. The toxins and bad energy struggle to escape your body, but you hold them in, embrace the darkness like... a lover. Now it has formed this... this *car*buncle. Here wait..."

Equinox pulled one of his Gold-Nuggets bubblegum sacks from his sporran and wandered the store randomly opening things – herbs, soap powders, liquids, grated cheese – pouring portions of their contents into his little sack, then returning the opened products to the shelves. He walked back and stuffed the sack into Gator's shirt pocket, poking it several times, forcing it in deep.

"There. My gift to you. Apply this before bed and you will find... what you want. *In-your-dreams*."

Equinox went to Katy at the counter and touched her hand. She flinched and he went on, "So, everyone's going out to celebrate our nation's birth tonight? I guess I'd like to go see what that's all about... That'd be great fun, right, my love?"

She didn't respond and Equinox dropped his head almost to the counter to look back up into her face and said, "I didn't *hear* you... *Right*?"

Katy clenched her eyes, followed by a spasm of short, vigorous nods.

"Well, until then..." Equinox went on, rising back up. "I know you'll take good care of my woman... my lovely *wife*... until she returns *home*...to me... "

131

Frankenstein's Paradox

Katy pulled her shoulders together as he drew her to his side with a flexed arm while looking at Gator. The medicine man leaned in to kiss her. She squinted like someone anticipating an explosion, then he turned and left. No rolling, no hateful glares. It was all understood. He simply hit the door, walked out and was gone before it closed.

Neither of them had said a word during Equinox's performance.

They continued to stand in their places, not speaking.

***

It was cooler than it had been. It was still warm, but it was cooler.

The sun was falling down when Gator arrived at the bait shop and the brief shower that morning had done little to break the drought: by mid-day it had all dried up. There was parched irritability in the air.

It was the Fourth, but it was also a Monday, so the band was off and the jukebox played all night, which suited Gator just fine: he would not be thinking about the pedal steel player. Jim Reeves was on the Seeburg singing about a red-eyed and rowdy drinker who would be visiting folks and doing favors: the rarest of drunks; the ivory-billed woodpecker of inebriates. But it was good to be thinking of a pleasant and charitable man when Katy Lemonade entered with her odious, counter-paladin consort, whose poncho, headband, and cowrie-shell necklace trappings of a non-violent guru camouflaged the... it would be unfair to wolves to make the comparison.

Gator sat at the bar speaking with the welder Arbuthnot, whose big as a barn frame occluded his view, and the couple had crossed the room to meet them before he was aware they had come upon him. Gator had barely begun to mouth words of greeting when Vernal Equinox announced with lofty disdain that he did not poison his body, therefore spirit, with alcohol and would just partake of the pure spring (tap) water he had brought with him in a leather bota, but that Katy was, *of course,* free to make her own decisions. She asked for a glass of soda water then clutched it with both hands and looked nervously around the room. Equinox looked at Gator and Gator looked at Katy who, even in the neon light of the bar, appeared to have a contusion developing below her eye, and his mouth began to dry up.

Between quickening breaths Gator asked how she was. She merely nodded with a knitted brow and forcing a strained smile so patently counterfeit as to appear to be pulled from the corners of an unwilling mouth by invisible fingers.

"We're in perfect harmony... totally in tune," Equinox interjected on her behalf, looking down at her and snugging her up to his side like a buddy. She seemed more hostage than mate. Gator's frangible equilibrium began to strain and cleave. He swilled the last belt of backwash in his can and turned to order another when the vibrato Farfisa organ of "I Can Help" began to play. Equinox detected something in the brief glance Katy and Gator exchanged, then Katy suddenly exclaimed, "I want a beer!" pulling away from Equinox. "I want... I want a... a *Coors!*"

Gator called out, "Loaded up an' truckin'!" and held up two fingers to Charlene Williams, working her night job behind the bar. She nodded and reached down into the cooler for the recently fashionable bootleg brew.

"I love this song... I wanna dance!" Katy went on, looking straight at Gator. He wanted to, this time. But he knew that now she was – that *they* were – provoking something dangerous.

"Let's jus' sit an'... talk" he said cautiously.

"I want to do what *I* want to do..." she insisted and pointed straight up into the air right as Billy Swan sang,

"I got two strong arms
I can help... "

Charlene fumbled with the Coors' unfamiliar opening tabs and handed them to Gator, who handed one to Katy. Vernal, sandbagged by Katy's defiance and, for once, uncertain as to how to regain control, just stood massaging his city water-filled wineskin as Katy and Gator clinked their cans.

"Can't really... clank... with that thing... can ya?" Gator yelled over the music, redirecting Equinox's attention away from Katy and poking at Vernal's flaccid sac with his hard, dripping, sixteen ounce can. *"Just sorta... squishy..."* he said flippantly, *"doesn't really... CLANG,"* accentuating the onomatopoeia with a short punching motion.

Katy snorted half her beer and held the back of her hand against her nose. She looked Gator square in the eye and again demanded, "I wanna *dance!*"

Vernal Equinox abruptly took Katy Lemonade by the arm to pull her away. Gator stood up but Katy looked over her shoulder and shook her head, "No," as she was dragged off. She jerked her arm away but accompanied Equinox, unresisting, to the corner by the pay phone. At first the conversation appeared calm, Equinox at times seemed even supplicating. Gator sat back down but could see now

133

their conversation grew more heated. He stood back up. Equinox began to gesticulate wildly, at one point thumping his chest with his open palm and Gator's blood began to heat like water in a pipe beneath a propane torch. The logic of what this would mean for Gator if he acted was subsumed by his single desire to rescue Katy from her Hell. Equinox slammed the wall with the side of his fist. Katy spoke back aggressively and in the light of the cigarette machine Gator could see her say, "Go *fuck* yourself." The pressure built as his blood nearly boiled like a pocket trapped by ice.

Then, Vernal Equinox slapped Katy Lemonade across the face: twelve – O – one. The pipe burst and Gator was on Equinox before he could recoil his fist.

Vernal went across a table and into the shuffleboard as a group of drinkers scattered. But Equinox was no pushover or stranger to violence and was immediately wrestling with Gator, who Equinox slammed into the jukebox.

Katy began to scream, "Stop! *Stop! NO!*"

But they wrestled until, when forced back against the leech tank, Vernal lost his balance and fell in. Gator took advantage, grabbing him by the poncho and forced his head into the bubbling tub of pond scum and blood-sucking worms. As Vernal burbled, Katy continued to plead, brokenheartedly, "Gator... *No...* not this... they'll take you..."

Gator pulled the gasping Vernal Equinox from the tank and scolded, "*If ya know you're a BEAST...*" then returned him to the tank, only to finish his message – one that Vernal never truly understood – through a series of repeated dunkings and retrievals,

brbrbrrllgglrburbul!
gasp!
"Chain"
bbbllrrgglrburblle!
gasp!
"Your "
brurglebubblurbleglub!
gasp!
"Self"
gubrglrburblrglubglub!
gasp!
"Ta"
burgblubgrurgleblurp!
gasp!
"The Ra-Di-A-Tor!!!"

Arbuthnot swooped in and swept Gator up with an arm big as a Christmas ham and away from the tank. Gator dropped the soaked and still gasping Vernal to the floor and as they dragged him away to the bar, heaving, he turned around to see Katy, but she was already walking... away – back to Equinox.

"Git 'im outta here, Francis!" Charlene Williams commanded Arbuthnot. "*Quick like!!*"

Arbuthnot pulled the emotionally drained Gator to the door who turned once more back to Katy, tugging on a leech that hung from Equinox's lobe like a pendant earring, and Gator pulled at the massive paw that held him. Arbuthnot paused, sensing his yearning. Gator weakly uttered, "I got two strong arms..." was then dragged away, and realized he would never see her again.

Two men came in as the pair neared the door. They looked around at the scene and asked what was going on. Arbuthnot motioned with his head back towards Vernal Equinox, said, "Freak accident..." and they left the place to only the sound of crickets and the jukebox 45 repeating, "Don't forget me baby..."

The moon had not yet risen when Gator drove down Mill Spring Road to his home but he could tell something was different. When he neared the end, he saw there was only a smoking hole where the Duquesne twin's house had been. Nobody needed to explain that this was collateral damage of the insect wars: the unintentional, yet inevitable precipitate yield of petroleum, alcohol and bottle rockets. He climbed out of the Capri and stood looking at the smoldering ruin across the driveway, so far from the road, or a phone, or civilization, that no one had even been aware it had burned.

"Finally gart rid a 'em warsps."

Gator jumped, not realizing that Marie had silently materialized at his side.

"Good riddance ter tha' 'ere house," she went on. "Been nothin' but a curs'ed place since 'at girl died a th' saturnism back in Eisna-how'r."

"Where's the brothers?" Gator asked, feeling the thing in his shirt pocket and pulling it out.

"Jackrabbited..." said Marie.

Gator worked Vernal's poultice around in his hand. Marie took it from him and studied it.

"'At from 'at 'ere root doctor what live in th'Injun hut down bah th'river?"

Gator nodded and realized he would never know half of what went on in Marie's life.

"His'ns caterplasms ain't useful..." she ruled and tossed the bootless plaster to the weeds.

"Yeah... Well... I'm headin' on," Gator mournfully sighed, then gave Marie a little salute and said, "Tomorrow..."

"Yessir..." Marie repeated, "they a-done a-tooked off..."

Gator stopped on the stairs and looked at the smoking shell, "Yeah... Poor dumbfu-... Poor buddy pegs,"

"Ain't no shame in a-runnin," she said softly.

Gator turned back to Marie and lingered on her glistening eyes. He smiled and said, "Goodnight, Marie," and went up the stairs and inside.

"Goodbye, Gater."

***

VIII

JD Hollingsworth

It all happened that quickly. Now it was all over.

Roosevelt Delano "Gator" Franklin lay in the dark on his floor staring at the ceiling and chain smoking. His life *was* essentially over. He knew that.

"Sometimes..." he thought, "ya try ta get out a somethin'... try *reallll* real hard... but... don't quite make it. Sometimes, maybe, the tunnel... jus' needed ta be a few yards longer. Ya know... You're... You're still inside a the wire..."

He took a long French inhale on his cigarette, held it, then let out a long cloud of smoke and whispered, "But ya don't know 'til ya come up."

No one ever knows until they come up.

He thought that in the end his brain had somehow won. Gator had tried, but it – whatever "it" was – punched him in the jaw for wanting what he believed was supposed to be. Whatever it was: his hindbrain, his brainstem, his amygdala, hypothalamus, squeezin's, offal... whatever, something *supposedly* in his brain, and he didn't know, they didn't know, no one knew what happened back there.

He *had* tried but, in the end, he couldn't control what had forced him to act. But the act – the action he took – was, he felt, one of nobility. Violent, yes, but he had acted to protect someone he loved – even if she would never know it – from a brute, a monster. A different monster: the real criminal in this.

But that didn't matter. This was just the last link in his chain of stupidity and they would be coming for *him* for sure, and he would be going back to that place. And he would never see her again. And most agonizing of all: there would be no one to watch over her. And the beast would still be out there.

It was all going to be so different, he thought, "It is different... they've made it different." He could hardly contain his agony and sadness. He lay there and tensed his stomach to hold it in.

"*Why...?*"

After months of the Duquesne's tearing up the place across the road, Gator's ears could now, as a result of the brother's self-immolation, again hear silence and the small things that hid within it and, as he lay there, full of pain, he heard a rustle and another noise: an almost human noise – almost – but he could not tell what it was. He sat up and looked out the front window to see a strange shadow – large, hulking – lurking in the untended brush of the yard and his hair stood on end.

Gator was a rational man, a scientist at heart. But a man of reason, confronted with a manifestation from beyond reason, the otherworldly, the fantastic, the numinous made real, is filled with a terror more profound, more darkly primeval, than that of the credulous. The boreal chorus of insects and rain crows became silent and he heard a wet, feral grunt. He saw the big, top-heavy silhouette fumble strangely in the shadows.

"Nooo...It's... it's the..." Gator said, his heart racing. "It... can't...*be*."

And then a blood-curdling, gurgling, "Whoooooooo!" howled from the darkness.

The beast fumbled again in some hand play of unknown purpose, and its green eyes began to glow.

"My *god!!!*... just like they..."

The eyes dimmed but a small orange sprite remained for a moment, glowing and dancing around the head of the inter-dimensional primate, then it too dimmed. Once more, there was a grunt, and its green eyes flashed, one, two, three times, and there was a strange, repeating scratching, like the stridulation of the now silent insects. There was grunt, another scratching sound and the eyes glowed again – bright and green – then, again, they went dark.

For a moment all was silent and still and dark.

Gator, looked from side to side and to the back of the house. He was safe inside the house. But then, only the screen door was closed. And where would he go if he did dash out the back? What if it just walked *in* the door??

Another fierce and frustrated cry yowled from outside: mere feet from where he sat hunched below the window frame. Trying to close the door would only alert it to his presence.

Again, a grunt. He peeked above the sill in time to see, almost face-to-face, the thing's green eyes glow and he dropped like a startled chipmunk back to his hiding place.

If he could get to Marie, she had that Confederate pistol.

"No, wait!" he remembered, "She said she *knows* him... Maybe she could talk ta... *Jesus*. What the hell am I talkin' about?"

Gator trembled, then heard, another grunt, an angry growl, then, "This a..." huff "This a-heyah Zippo... piece a *SHIT!*"

snort

"Jesus...What th'..." Gator exhaled, slightly relieved. "Is that...!?"

Gator raised back up to look out and watched a shirtless Anderson, now outside the shrubbery and more visible in the rising moon, lurch around, aimlessly snorting and whooping. He bent his big head down, again attempting to re-light his failed cigarette. As Anderson shielded the lighter from the wind and pulled over and over on the butt, Gator saw the Zippo's pulsing reflection off of Anderson's glasses through the green plastic visor in his hat's brim.

And then Gator knew... Anderson *was* the Spring Valley Ape...

"I mean... *right?*"

"What time is it?" Gator now asked himself aloud. He got up to look at the kitchen clock. "Eleven forty, Christ!"

Anderson raised his arms above his head, like someone praising Jesus at a camp meeting, and bellowed "Whoooooo hoooo. H'yeah! Hooooooo!"

"I'll be *God* damned!"

A quarter mile away Everett Lawson was arriving early for his shift at the Adair Heartland Corporation's Dixie Feed Mills to begin his rounds as he had, five nights a week, for the past twenty-three years...

Gator yelled out the screen door, "What the fuck are you doin' in my goddamn yard in the middle a the fuckin' night, Anderson?"

"Yo yahd!? This mah yahd ya... ya li'uhl ass-ho... An' yo frens done" slurp "done BUHN'ED mah HOUSE down."

Gator felt his rage begin, then thought of Poshlost in a rain of books. He calmed a bit and said "I pay rent so that makes it mine..." and he thought about his situation, then added, "For now..."

...Lawson crossed the gravel yard from the main office to Elevator #4 where he walked the floor...

"*Bool*-shit froot pah..." slurp "Pays up own rent tahm fo' *MAH* PRAH-puh-ty." huff "An' I be hyeah braht'n'erleh, pick-it-*UP!* Eh-vuh-ruh month."

Gator popped the screen door and stepped outside to face Anderson. He paused, breathed and thought, "...fallin' shelves, standards ripped from the wall, books bouncin' off of Poshlost's bald head..." then trod one step at a time down the stairs and saw that the bare-chested Anderson had a massive bruise on his hip, and the beefy arm he dragged across his chin to wipe the drippings had a bandage wrapped around it.

"...An' yooo bettah not be a-droppin' them PANG PUNG bawls on mah floah!!" snort huff

... then Lawson returned to the gravel lot outside where he ran into Charlie Dobson ...

Anderson retrieved his penis and began to urinate as Gator emerged.

... and he and Lawson shared a smoke and talked about the Braves...

"Aggghhh... Man... why do ya keep burnin' me like that, man? Put that thing away," Gator complained, finally addressing Anderson's withered genitals.

"Buhnin' ya?... Whooooo hooo" snort smack "you some kinda crazeh froot boah..."

Gator thought of an endless torrent, a waterfall, a Niagara of books and shelves and standards and brackets.

slurp "You some kindah froot wi' yah *uhhhhhbs*" huff "an' yah fancy book a-readin' an' yah..."

... Lawson and Dobson finished their smokes, agreed that kid Murphy looked okay if they would give him a shot, and went their separate ways...

"Yeah, sure, okay whatever ya..." Gator snarled as the coping device began to give at the edges, and thought, but didn't say, "... fat sack a shit!"

...Lawson entered Elevator #3...

"Whu' th'... whu' th' shit you a-smilin' foah? Whoooo! Yoa ah damn *froot*. Whooo! You an' alla yah..."

... where he then went into the little glassed-in office by the bathroom hallway with the sprinkler control valves for the adjoining storage warehouse and underground passages...

Gator thought so hard on the damage to Poshlost's office wall that he could *smell* the sulfurous aroma of shattered sheetrock.

... where Lawson picked up a Playboy magazine and flipped through...

"Gonna get mah *LAW*-yah an' mah nigguh an' throw *yo* frooty ass out on th-"
SMACK!
Socking Anderson in the mush didn't come with the satisfaction that hitting a normal man would have. His gin-blossomed, edema-blobbed face flab absorbed the blows so that hitting him had no more gratifying effect than pounding a lump of pizza dough, but now a battle in the emerging moonlight erupted, which quickly devolved into sloppy Greco-Roman grappling.

...Lawson decided go to the bathroom but paused for a few more glances at Patti McGuire...

Anderson was old, but large and powerful, and – with his persistent drooling and sweating – just touching his slick, clammy skin evoked the same shivery revulsion as handling a handful of the bait shop's nightcrawlers or a much-slobbered-on dog toy. All of this, and that Anderson's penis was still out and flopping around, made Gator cautious in his grappling, which all led to it being very nearly an equal match.

... Lawson walked to the darkened hallway where he groped for the faulty light switch he kept meaning to report to the facilities manager. He thought, "gotta tell Bamhill in the morning," then, hampered by his missing forefinger, he swatted unsuccessfully at the switch several times.

Then Gator stopped, stepped back, looked the ancient beast in the eye and cried, "No!... "

Frustrated, he stopped swatting then carefully began to run his hand up the wall towards the switch plate

"No," Gator said again, "Stop... Cool it... Truce" then he whispered, almost soothingly, to the Ape, "No..." then, raising his hands, again whispered, "This is... This is not the time..."

and flicked the toggle of the shorting circuit...

huff snort

One minute past midnight of July 5th, 1977, Elevator #3 of the Adair Heartland Corporation's Dixie Feed Mills bulged for a nanosecond, then blew apart in a chain-reaction of incinerating microscopic corn particles. The resulting shockwave, arriving seconds before any warning sound, dropped the old skyrocket water tower, which flopped to the earth where its pointy cap blew off and its rusty rivets popped, launching a torrent of collected rainwater which, with its load of spring peeper polliwogs, spilled to flood across Marie's yard and drain into the ditch, refreshing the drought-starved spring.

The peepers ceased to peep.
The bugs in the trees did not know which way to call it.

The moon hung like a slice of bone on the night.

***

IX

JD Hollingsworth

It rained for three weeks after "the Blast."

***

In the winter following the infamous "Leech Tank Lickin'," Katy moved out of Vernal Equinox's cornstalk-insulated wigwam, filed a restraining order, filed for divorce and moved into a shotgun shack on Railroad Avenue.

Finding that her clapboard home was easily violated, after coming home to find the door kicked in and "BITCH!" painted on her walls, she moved to a renovated garage of brick with a steel door. This proved inviolable: only once having her kitchen window pried open with a running garden hose pushed through.

Still, the streets were unguarded and one night at her doorstep the harmless and loving ninety pound girl was yanked to the curb by the one hundred and eighty pound bogus medicine man – who each day rode a bicycle ten miles with a rucksack full of stones – to begin a savage punishment for the crime of rejecting his magnificence. The blows had only begun to rain down when a larger, stronger, pair of arms pulled the sham man from Katy Lemonade, curled in the dirt, lifting him fully into the air, then popping Vernal's shoulder from its socket, as Hashim Abdulsalam Batal Azil flung him to the ground with the bitter taste of his own discredited medicine in his mouth – a mouth which screamed like a baby at the pain of his dislocation.

Azil carried the frightened girl inside and calmed her, then, certain that he would once more be accused of a crime he did not commit, *and* be found in the home of a brutalized white woman, he attempted to flee. But Katy in her fright and need for the nearness of a kind person begged him to stay. In the end the former Jericho Milton finally saw justice done as the star witness for the ultimate conviction of one Vernon B. Higglebutts, formerly of Phenix City, Alabama, who, three months later in the Georgia State Prison at Reidsville, as a newly recruited member of the Aryan Forrest Knights, became cellmate of the incoming Rail Road Duquesne.

Certain they were wanted for arson, (but, within days of their disappearance following the fire, most certainly were for parole violation) Rifleman and Rail Road Duquesne had remained in hiding in the brambly woods near the family property on Rangle's Branch for almost a year. After being ratted out by a brother, just for fun, they had set out to escape and had escaped Torcall County by stealing John Anderson's still-garaged Mercedes. Once into Ford County they, stupidly and unsurprisingly, stopped for beer at the Majik Market. The filthy and bearded figures piqued the interest of Sheriff Burstyn, there buying coffee and a Slim Jim, particularly as they traveled in a large and golden Mercedes sedan having once belonged to the true, but unknown, Spring Valley Ape. The sheriff walked out to question the hermit twins and a high-speed pursuit ensued.

As Rail Road explains,

"S'*fuuucked* up, bro! Sheriff come a-haulin' ass up on us an' ol' Rifle a-starts jus' a-*freakin'* out an' run ar own ass offa th' *fuh*-kin' road lak a dumbass an' we ends up *UP*-fuckin'-side fuckin'-*DOWN* down th' fuckin' ditch so's we cain't n'even open th' fuckin' doors, but th' back winda 'ere done blowed out an' we crawls our ass outta 'ere lookin' lak fuckin' *cave*men an' Ah runs one a-way an' Rifle he run off down th' fuckin' middla th' fuckin' road an' a big ass fuckin' truck come 'long an' ol' Rifle, he run one a-way an th'other an' gets over't th' fuckin' side okay, *THEN*... fucker doubles-back squirrel-style an' gets 'is ass fuckin' squarshed by 'at dang ol' honey wagon an' 'at fat ol' fuckin' sheriff by 'en he's a-standin' 'er an' he's jus' a-fuckin' *laaaa*-ffin' 'is fat ass off, an' I figger 'cuz

JD Hollingsworth

Rifle got squarshed by a shit truck fer bein' a dumbass an' all, ya know, but 'en he says 'I din't know 'ere'uz TWO fuckin' Apes' an,' shit, I reckon thad'uz kinda funny."

So, returned to Reidsville, alone, the irrational, if not transcendental, Rail Road regained his old status as inmate #314159 and missed his brother and, now and then, stood in front of his cell's stainless steel mirror just to see Rifleman again and, now and then, folded his hands up to the mirror, to wordlessly ask, "ELSTUFKC," and softly whisper, "*Yes*... buddy peg."

With no neighbors to regale, Marie could only rant of witnessing "Kang Kung an' Gargleziller a-battlin' in ther moonlight" to frightened, if doubtful, strangers, even as the defeated water tank lay as mute testament to the overweight reptile's well-known vendetta against infrastructure. And forget about trying to convince scurrying shoppers at the Food Bag to listen of how – what she claimed to be – a new dog, Pungo One, had blown out of a chicken noodle can on the night of "the Blast," and how she said, "'Ah's a-gonna name you WILLIE!' an' he a-says, 'NO!' He a-says 'my name be *Pungo One*!' SO, I says, 'Okay. Who m'Ah ta tell a dog?'"

In the fullness of time Marie Woodley passed and, for a while, kept Pungo One nourished until he too went to his reward.

After all, who *was* she to tell a dog?

With none to care, Anderson's and Marie's adjoining properties were eventually foreclosed upon and sold in non-judicial tax sales by the sheriff to Wal-Mart Stores Inc. whose regional superstore built there would remain open only long enough to drive the downtown shops of Utinahica out of business and whose engineers and contractors who came to survey the properties found in Gator's home only an ashtray, a yoga mat, and a shower of colorful paper as the tens of collages and scores of magazines, shredded for a hundred nests of a thousand rodents, rained down over them upon poking the overhead acoustic tiles, and who, after having hacked through the persistent florabunda, by then almost completely obscuring Marie's house like a passion flower and strangler-fig smothered Mayan ruin, discovered therein the mummified remains of a human, and a dog, and an empty wingback chair, in which once had sat a large and very life-like doll – or not – yet, with none to know this, there were none to wonder where, or how, it had gone.

Frankenstein's Paradox

The earth being scraped away by the machinery was sent off for fill on other projects here and there until the local amateur anthropologist – with little to do after Ape sightings to investigate and spoor samples to collect and catalog had mysteriously ceased – filed suit for a stop-order on the project, claiming it to be an ancient burial ground. Though it was on private land, the project was temporarily halted while lawyers parsed the language of the Georgia Code, Section 12-3-53 paragraphs 3 and 5 to see if it even applied. Before this was resolved, the courts allowed the work to proceed: there being, whether the code applied or not, no evidence whatsoever of any archeological value. So, when the skyrocket water tower was finally dismantled and craned away and the area beneath it was cleared and loaded onto big trucks and bones were seen in the dirt of the backhoe's drop and then among the kudzu and pebbles in the steel beds, the foreman who was called over to investigate, simply, and furiously, harangued the workers that he wasn't going to hold this up for any "goddamned Indian shit," told them to pull out the vines and send the soil, along with its skeletal inclusions, on its way "before any hippies sees it."

Therefore, in the end, it was determined that five known Utinahican humans had perished – along with an unknown number of pets, livestock and forest inhabitants of various species – in the Blast.

Everett Lawson was, miraculously, not one.

Some also speculated that it was the demise of The Ape or that it had scared him from the land. One way or another the Ape moved on and was never to be seen or heard in the forest or among the Mills again.

Mrs. John Anderson had made her home-going shortly before the Blast. Their only child had vanished under mysterious and horrifying circumstances as a boy, taking the old woman's heart and the old man's decency with it. No one missed his father or her husband.

And Gator Franklin? Folks around figured he had just lammed out to avoid the rap he was about to take.

If they wondered at all.

***

Well, Katy did.

She wondered after she had drawn the new smiley face-covered help-wanted sign.

She wondered after the going-out-of-business sign she had drawn after that – with sad faces, but still with peace signs and flowers.

She wondered just as she had wondered why Gator had suddenly become sad, distant and cold to her after that night she had thought they came so close at Miss Her: the night she had dropped a friend off across the road from him and had thought of stopping by but thought better of it and went home lonely and wanting.

She wondered even long, long after she had moved far, far away to roller-skate along 9W through Saugerties, and it made her tender hippie heart ache.

***

"...*What was that Burt said...? Lewis said?   ...* " it wondered, "...*'You don't beat it... You don't beat this river...?'*"

***

So, with plenty of water and plenty of oil, the red International Harvester R190 dump truck rolled away down the Fitzgerald Road with its load of dirt and bones. It turned onto 138 then onto 441 and rumbled through the nice autumn day as its driver sang merrily along with his 8-track,

When I go to sleep at night, you're always a part of my dream...
  Holdin' me tight, an' tellin' me
    eeee'vahry-thing
      I wanna hear!
  Don't forget me baby...

The big truck pulled onto 280, passing through Mt. Vernon and Vidalia and from there to Reidsville, where *What was I* had briefly existed, had always know why Rail Road was "Pie," and now, somewhere, recalled Paul Muni's dump truck escape.

Frankenstein's Paradox

The truck turned north, on through Cobbtown and Metter, where everything's better, and on through the woods, up beyond the fall-line, and where that road ended began up a bigger gravel road where it stopped, backed up, and, just after noon and a few halting jerks, its big telescoping hydraulic cylinder began to slowly raise the bed.

Don't forget me baby...

What was I, victim, victor, indifferently considered clod of matter subject to the motive and the constraining laws of Man and Nature – the sausage laws – finally began to move up.

Don't forget me baby ...

What was I, a collage of experience untethered to a rememberer, would not forget.

Don't forget me baby ...

What was I – even before they had begun to slide down the steel bed – had calculated the coefficient of friction of the fungible pebbles and the granular soil moving towards the truck's swinging gate

Don't forget me baby...

What was I would soon pass through, to tumble gently down a sloping berm on the construction road for the powerful machines working to hold back the waters of the Okgatalatchee on the Lake Erskine Caldwell dam.

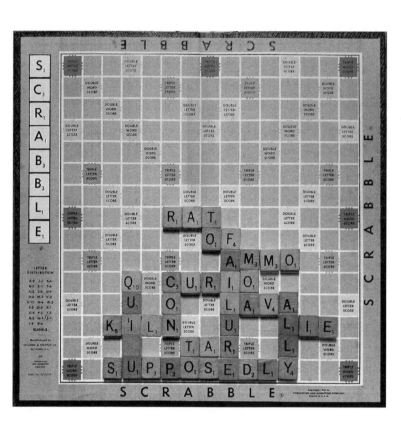